TAYLOR-MADE TALES

THE COWGIRL'S LUCK

TAYLOR-MADE TALES

THE COWGIRL'S LUCK

by

ELLEN MILES

AN
APPLE
PAPERBACK

SCHOLASTIC INC.

New York London Toronto Auckland Sydney
Mexico City Hong Kong New Delhi Buenos Aires

ISBN 0-439-59710-2

12 11 10 9 8 7 6 5 4 3 2 1   6 7 8 9 10 11/0

Printed in the U.S.A.   40

First printing, October 2006

For Kristin,
with love and thanks

TAYLOR-MADE TALES

THE COWGIRL'S LUCK

The Shy Girl

Me! Me!" The classroom was a forest of waving hands. Every kid in the room was shouting at once. Mr. Taylor was about to start a new story. A Taylor-Made Tale. Molly could hardly wait. But she didn't shout or wave her hand. Molly sat quietly, the way she always did. It didn't make sense to wave your hand if you didn't want the teacher to call on you.

A few months ago, nobody in room 3B would have known what a Taylor-Made Tale even *was*. Back then, Mrs. Nelson was their teacher. She read to them every afternoon, but it was always from a book. Molly had loved Mrs. Nelson. She was comfy and nice and she gave good hugs and never, never yelled.

At first, Molly had been a little afraid of Mr. Taylor. He was so tall and skinny, and his eyebrows were so bushy. He didn't yell, but he wasn't a big hugger, either. You never knew quite what to expect from Mr. Taylor.

But Mr. Taylor could do something that no other teacher in the world could do. You could name any five items, no matter how weird or mismatched they were, and he could make a story out of them. That was a Taylor-Made Tale. Every story ended up in the big red notebook that sat on Mr. Taylor's desk. And every student in room 3B was going to get a chance to name the five items.

That was why they were waving their hands. They all wanted the next story to be *their* story. Cricket and Leo had already had their chances, but they both had their hands up anyway.

"Actually, I think it's Molly's turn." Even though Molly was the only one who wasn't yelling or waving her hand, Mr. Taylor was looking straight at her. And smiling.

Oh, no! Molly stared back at her teacher. *My* turn?

Molly felt her face get hot. Whenever her cheeks tingled like that, she knew she was blushing. She hated that. She started to say something, but her voice was a squeak. Molly stopped and blushed some more. She wished she could sink into the floor like the wicked witch in *The Wizard of Oz*, leaving nothing but a medium-sized Molly puddle to show where she had been sitting.

Molly Hamilton was the shy girl.

Just like Jennifer Tourville was the popular girl, and Leo Murray was the class clown, Molly, with her long brown braids and thin, serious face, was the shy girl.

Everybody knew it. And it seemed like they'd never let her forget it.

Since her days at Patsy's Place Preschool, she'd been hearing her classmates describe her to their friends. "That's Molly. She's the shy girl."

Oliver had said it to Mr. Taylor on his first day. "Don't call on Molly too much," Oliver had said. "She's shy."

"Molly's a little shy," her mother had said a million times, to explain why Molly was hiding behind a chair (when she was two) or not taking part in a piano recital (last month).

And it was true. Molly *was* shy. She wasn't the kind of kid who would plop down next to you in the cafeteria and ask what was in your lunch bag. She'd never wanted to be the star of the class play — or even to be *in* the class play. Even answering an easy math problem could make her heart pound, her palms sweat, and her knees melt.

The only place Molly wasn't shy was at home, with her brothers (there were three of them, all older) and her parents.

There were days that Molly wanted to be more than just the shy girl. Being the shy girl was — well, it was kind of boring. Molly knew she was smart, and funny, and good at things. She could draw a horse that really looked like a horse, for example, or count to twenty in Japanese. But nobody knew. All they knew was that Molly was shy.

"Mr. Taylor! Molly doesn't even *want* her turn!" Jason yelled. "Can I go?"

Molly looked over at Jason Tourville, Jennifer's twin brother. As usual, he was wearing his Shaq jersey. Jason's five items would probably all be about basketball since that was practically all he ever thought about lately.

Mr. Taylor raised his eyebrows at Molly. "Is that true?" he asked. "You don't want your turn?"

Molly blushed. "Yes!" she said. "I mean, no! It's not true. I do want my turn." She looked down at her desk, avoiding Jason's glare.

In fact, she couldn't wait for her turn. She had been thinking about which five things she would choose ever since Mr. Taylor had told his first tale. It was the part about being called on that was hard. Being called on meant she had to speak in front of the class, and that meant she would stumble on her words and blush and feel like an idiot.

"Good!" said Mr. Taylor. "So, what will it be? What five things do you want your story to be about?"

Molly squinched her eyes shut for a second, making sure she remembered all five items. Then she took a deep breath. "A star," she said. "A penny, heads up. A white pony, a magic kettle, and a pair of golden scissors." She only stumbled twice, once on *pony* and once when she had to pause for another quick breath.

"Whoa!" said Jennifer. "Cool list!"

Molly felt her cheeks getting hot again. Would she ever be able to stop blushing all the time? She gave Jennifer a quick glance and a tiny smile. She was glad somebody else thought her list was good. She was sure it was going to turn into a great story. A fairy tale, her favorite kind.

It would be a story where wishes on stars came true and where people picked up lucky pennies and made their fortunes a day later. A story with a magic kettle that would make two of everything you put into it, and a pair of golden scissors that could turn a few yards of silk into a ball gown in two seconds.

And the pony? Well, in Molly's family, horses were lucky. When they were on a long car trip, they always played a game where they tried to spot horses and ponies. A white pony was the very best type you could spot. It guaranteed not only a hundred points, but good luck for the rest

of the trip, too. And a white pony would fit perfectly in a fairy tale.

Molly sat back in her chair, looking up at Mr.
Taylor. He nodded and smiled. "Wonderful!"
he said. "That's the story about Jessie and the
big spring roundup. I didn't know you liked
cowboys."

"Cowboys?" Molly asked.

Cowboys???

What do cowboys have to do with anything?" Molly blurted out, forgetting for the moment about being shy. She didn't particularly like cowboys. She didn't dislike them, either. She just didn't really think about them much.

"They have everything to do with the story you asked for," said Mr. Taylor with a little shrug.

Molly couldn't figure out how cowboys could be part of a fairy tale. "But . . ." she began.

"Just let him tell the story," said Jason. "It sounds great to me. I love cowboys."

"Did you hear the one about the cowboy who got a dachshund?" Leo asked.

Molly knew a joke was coming. Leo had a joke for every topic. "Why did he do that?" she asked gamely.

"Because someone told him to get a long little dogie," Leo said. He laughed so hard that he snorted a little.

"Ha-ha," said Oliver, pushing up his glasses. "I like astronauts better than cowboys, myself. But I also like Mr. Taylor's stories, no matter what they're about."

"Me, too!" yelled Cricket.

"Okay," Molly said meekly. What else could she do?

"Great!" said Mr. Taylor. "Let's get started." Everybody jumped up to follow him as he took three long steps over to the reading corner. He folded his long body into the big green easy chair with the worn corduroy cover. And then, as Molly and the other kids got settled, Mr. Taylor reached up to turn on the lamp.

Molly loved the lamp Mr. Taylor had brought to their classroom. It had a painted shade with different scenes on every side. This time, she noticed a picture she hadn't seen before, of a small figure astride a horse. The two were just shadows against a wide-open landscape of prairies and mountains, so Molly couldn't tell what color the horse was. Still, the picture gave her a happy little shiver. Maybe Oliver was right. Any story Mr. Taylor told would be good. Even if it was about cowboys.

Molly grabbed a yellow-and-orange-striped pillow and sat down near Mr. Taylor's chair. Once everybody was quiet, the teacher smiled at the circle of faces looking up at him. Then he took a deep breath and began.

■ ■ ■

"Bet you can't rope that fence post from here," said Dexter.

"Bet I can," Jessie answered. She squinted at the post. Then, with movements that looked as natural to her as breathing, she raised her lasso and sent it spinning toward the post. The circle at the end of her rope drifted out, out, out and fell gently onto its target. "Bull's-eye!" she hooted, pulling hard on the rope to tighten the loop, as if the fence post were about to snort and bolt away like a wild young calf would.

"Nice going," said Dexter. "Now how about that . . ."

■ ■ ■

"Wait, wait, wait!" yelled Jennifer, interrupting Mr. Taylor in midsentence. "What's a lasso? Who's Jessie? What's going on?"

Molly sighed. Jennifer was so impatient! Molly knew that the story would unfold and that Mr. Taylor would explain everything in time. But not if they didn't let him tell it.

"A lasso," Mr. Taylor said calmly, "is a rope with a loop at one end. Cowboys use it to catch horses and cattle. A good roper can throw a lasso from a galloping horse and snag a cow that is running off, or a calf that needs branding, or even a wild mustang."

"Everybody knows that," Jason said disgustedly, poking his twin sister. "C'mon, let him tell the story."

"Maybe I should back up a bit and begin at the beginning," said Mr. Taylor. "Would that help?"

Jennifer crossed her arms and nodded. Her

bottom lip was sticking out. Jennifer was used to getting her way.

"Okay, let's start over," said Mr. Taylor. He leaned back in his chair, took a deep breath, and began the story — again.

Jessie's Story Begins

Once upon a time, way out in the Wild, Wild West, there was a girl named Jessie with beautiful long red hair that shone like a new penny, and a nose sprinkled with freckles. She lived on a ranch that was almost as big as most states back East. It was called the Rocking R Ranch, and Jessie had lived there all her life with her mother and father. Plus about two thousand head of cattle, fifty or so horses, and a dozen ranch hands — cowboys, that is.

Of course, the cattle didn't live in the ranch house. They were spread out all over the range, grazing on grass, and having calves, and living their lives while the cowboys watched over them.

Jessie loved living on a ranch. She loved everything about it: the creaking sound of the windmill that pumped their water; the smell of the leather bridles that her father repaired near the fireplace after supper; the way the stars were so thick and so bright at night you could see the outline of the mountain range to the west, just by their light.

And Jessie loved horses. Especially her pony Smokey, who was a pinto. That meant he was stocky and strong, with a white coat splotched with black.

■ ■ ■

"What?" Molly couldn't help it. The word just slipped out. "It was supposed to be a white pony," she mumbled. Mr. Taylor looked her way with raised eyebrows.

"Well, he's mostly white," said Mr. Taylor. "Will that do?"

By now, Molly knew she was blushing deep red. She just nodded. Of course it would do. Mr. Taylor was the best storyteller ever. If he said the pony was a pinto, it was a pinto.

Molly nodded, and Mr. Taylor went back to the story.

■ ■ ■

Jessie had been riding Smokey since they were both five years old. Now they were both twelve.

They'd grown up together, the two of them. By now, Jessie only had to think a command: *Forward! Let's go that way! Whoa!* before Smokey obeyed it.

That didn't mean he was always perfect. Sometimes Smokey could be a brat, with a mind of his own. Sometimes he liked to pretend he'd never heard the word *whoa.* Then he'd take Jessie on a wild, galloping ride across the open range.

"Give you a hundred dollars for that horse," Slim had said to Jessie more than once. Slim was a cowboy who had worked on the ranch for as long as Jessie could remember.

Of course, Jessie just laughed at the idea of selling Smokey. Why, she wouldn't sell him for a thousand dollars. She'd sooner sell Dexter.

■ ■ ■

"Dexter!" interrupted Jennifer. "What kind of name is Dexter?"

"Shhhh!" said everybody else. They were all leaning forward, listening to every one of Mr. Taylor's words.

Molly had already forgotten how much she'd wanted her story to be a fairy tale. She could tell that she was going to like Jessie, and she couldn't wait to find out more about her. If people kept interrupting, Mr. Taylor would never finish the story. She sighed, and then she frowned at Jennifer.

"What?" Jennifer asked when she heard Molly sigh. "All I asked was . . ."

"He'll explain everything," Jason told his sister. "Just be patient." He looked at Mr. Taylor. "Right?" he asked. "You were just about to explain about Dexter, weren't you?"

"Of course," said Mr. Taylor. He glanced at the clock on the wall. Molly's heart sank. Were they already out of time?

"We have a few more minutes. Plenty of time to meet Dexter." Mr. Taylor leaned back and went on with the story.

■ ■ ■

Dexter was Jessie's best friend. He lived over at the Double Bar T Ranch, about ten miles away. During the bitter winters, when work on the ranch was slow, he and Jessie did schooling together, with Jessie's mother. They learned about other countries and how children lived in Holland, and Japan, and Egypt. They added figures and practiced their spelling. And they worked on their penmanship, though Dexter never did get beyond what Jessie's mother called the chicken-scratch stage.

If there was a bad snowstorm, Dexter would stay overnight at the Rocking R, sleeping in the bunkhouse with the cowboys. Otherwise, he would ride back and forth between the ranches every day on his horse, Red.

That was winter.

In the other seasons, everything was different. Dexter helped his father and uncle run the Double Bar T, working alongside the men and doing everything they did, from roping to riding to doctoring sick cattle.

And Jessie knew how to do those things, too. She and Smokey could run down a calf and rope it as fast as any other horse and rider on both ranches. Jessie knew how to help a cow give birth, how to tie a knot so it would hold, how to build a campfire, and even how to climb like a monkey up the windmill when it needed fixing.

But Jessie didn't often have a chance to do all those things. Her father said she had other responsibilities on the Rocking R Ranch. He counted on her to help her mother with the cooking, the mending, and all the other things women did to make sure the home parts of the ranch ran as smoothly as the rest.

■ ■ ■

"Not fair!" yelled Jennifer.

"Yeah!" said Cricket, sitting up straight. "Girls can do everything boys can do."

"Well," said Mr. Taylor. "That's true, and that's the way people think nowadays. But back then, people saw things differently."

Molly kept quiet, as usual. She really wished that Jennifer would stop interrupting. But the truth was, she agreed with her friends. It wasn't fair. And the funny thing? Some people still thought like that. Like Molly's father, sort of. His idea of what girls couldn't or shouldn't do was a little old-fashioned, as Molly's mother would say.

But it wouldn't have helped to complain about

things not being fair. That was just how Molly's father was, and he wasn't going to change.

■ ■ ■

Jessie knew that there was no point in complaining, said Mr. Taylor. That was just the way her father was.

■ ■ ■

Molly stared at Mr. Taylor. Was he a mind reader? Or was it only a coincidence that Jessie's father was just like hers? The teacher caught her eye and gave her a little smile. Then he went on with the story.

■ ■ ■

Instead of complaining, Jessie worked hard to help her mother. The sooner the chores got done, after all, the sooner she could be back outside, practicing her roping or taking Smokey for a ride out to one of the far pastures.

On this particular clear, sunny day in early May, Jessie had helped her mother scrub the kitchen floor. They had also made three apple pies for that night's dessert (working cowboys had big appetites) and hung out a week's worth of laundry to dry in the chilly spring breeze.

When the laundry basket was empty, Jessie brought it back inside.

"Thank you, Jessie," said her mother, giving her a hug. "You're a great help. But you've done enough for today. I can see that look in your eye that says you need some time outdoors. There isn't much light left in the day. Go on, now!" She finished off her hug with a little shove.

Jessie stood out on the porch, shading her eyes against the low afternoon sun. She held her prized lasso loosely in one hand. The braided horsehair rope felt familiar, like an old friend.

"Hey!"

It was Dexter, riding up the ranch road astride his big roan horse, Red.

"Hey, yourself!" Jessie answered, jumping down off the porch. Lasso in hand, she ran for the corral. As she climbed onto the wooden fence, she clucked her tongue. Smokey was standing in his usual spot near an old mesquite tree, and he came trotting over as soon as he heard her. Jessie climbed off the fence and right onto Smokey's broad back.

Dexter had followed her to the corral. He jumped off Red in order to open the gate, led his horse through, and closed the gate. Then he climbed back up on Red, throwing his leg over the saddle.

He rode over to Jessie and Smokey. The two friends sat on their horses together, looking back toward the fence and the ranch house beyond.

"Bet you can't rope that fence post from here," said Dexter.

"Bet I can," Jessie answered. She squinted at the post. Then, with movements that were as natural to her as breathing, she raised her lasso and sent it spinning toward the post. The circle at the end of her rope drifted out, out, out and fell gently onto its target. "Bull's-eye!" she hooted, pulling hard on the rope to tighten the loop, as if the fence post were about to snort and bolt away the way a wild young calf would.

"Nice going," said Dexter. "Now how about the next one out?"

Jessie rode over to retrieve her lasso. Then she

rode back and threw it again, looping it around the farther post on the first try.

Jessie and Dexter threw rope after rope, challenging each other to hit smaller targets each time. Jessie felt perfectly happy sitting on Smokey's broad, warm back and soaking up the springtime sun.

Clang! Clang! Clang!

Jessie saw her mother standing on the porch of the ranch house. She was using a spoon to hit a big iron triangle that hung from one of the rafters. The dinner bell! It wasn't dinnertime yet, but maybe Ma had something tasty to offer them for a snack.

"How about some pie, you two?" called Ma.

Jessie and Dexter didn't hesitate. They slid off their horses and left them in the corral with pats and promises of carrots when they returned.

"You sure would be a big help at roundup," Dexter said as he and Jessie washed their hands at the pump that filled the watering trough by the windmill.

Jessie felt a twinge in her stomach. "Pa and the crew are heading out first thing tomorrow," she said. "I wish he'd let me come this year."

Spring roundup was one of the busiest times on the ranch. That was when all the hands at the ranch headed out to the farthest corners of the range shared by the nearby ranches. They looked for the new calves that had been born that winter and spring and branded them so everyone would know which ranch they belonged to. The cowboys would also round up the beef cattle that would be going to market, and drive them back to the ranch. It took days and days, and lots of men, to get all that done. It was hard work, but the cowboys had fun, too. They camped out at night and told stories and sang songs around the fire.

Jessie and Dexter headed into the warm, cozy kitchen of the ranch house, and Ma greeted them with plates of pie topped with cream from that morning's milking.

"When's the T crew heading out?" Ma asked Dexter. She knew it was roundup time for all the ranches.

"Not for a few days," Dexter said. "Our cook, Wiz, says his bones are aching from this chilly spring. He hasn't been able to get his chuck wagon all loaded up, and everybody knows roundup can't happen without plenty of chow. Pa said Wiz could hire a helper, so he's in town trying to find someone. " He took a big bite of his pie. "Mmm, that's good. We won't be having pie like that when we're out on the range."

Jessie felt that twinge again. Dexter was so lucky! He had gone on his first spring roundup two years ago, and by now he was considered one of the crew.

Ever since she could remember, Jessie had wanted to help with spring roundup. It was what she wished every time she blew out birthday candles, every time she found an eyelash that had fallen out, every time she spotted the first star in a darkening sky.

So far, that wish had never come true. But maybe this year would be different. Maybe this year her pa would decide she was old enough, and strong enough, and a good enough cowgirl. Maybe this year he'd shake her shoulder in the dark hours of the early morning and say, "Come on, Jess. Pack your bedroll, and let's hit the trail. You're coming on roundup."

The Contest

Mr. Taylor stretched his long arms overhead. "Well!" he said, looking around at the circle of faces that surrounded him. "Where has the time gone? If we don't hurry, you're going to be late for your library time, and I'll never hear the end of it from Ms. Wallace."

Molly gave her head a little shake. She was already so swept up in the story that she almost felt as if she were waking from a dream. She could *see* Jessie and Dexter sitting on their horses in the corral. She could picture Ma calling them to the table by banging on the iron triangle. And she could imagine just how badly Jessie wanted to go on that roundup.

She had completely forgotten about wanting a fairy-tale story for her tale. But she hadn't forgotten about her five items. So far, the only one that had appeared was Smokey, the pony. But Molly knew that the other four things would show up along the way as Mr. Taylor told the tale.

Mr. Taylor turned off the lamp and unfolded his long, tall body. "Okay, kiddos," he said. "Looks like we'll have to pick up Jessie's story tomorrow. She'll probably be waking up just around the same time you are, so think of her while you're brushing your teeth." He grinned. "If she's lucky, she'll be going on roundup!"

Molly thought about this as she and the rest of the class walked up the stairs and down the hall to the library. It wasn't fair! Good luck or not, Jessie should definitely be allowed to go on roundup. She knew how to do everything that Dexter could do.

Molly was so deep in thought that she didn't even notice when Leo and Cricket, who were walking right in front of her, suddenly stopped moving. "Oof!" she said as she bumped into Cricket. "Sorry!" Her face went all hot, and she looked down at the floor to avoid having to look at her classmates.

But they weren't paying attention to Molly. They were too busy looking at a big, bright orange poster.

SCHOOLWIDE HOOP SHOOT! it said in sort of drippy letters that made it look like somebody had put too much black paint on their brush. There were pictures of basketballs decorating the border of the poster. Most of them were sort of blobby, not perfectly round. Molly thought that a ball like that would take some pretty funny bounces.

Curious, Molly stepped closer, making sure not to step on Cricket's foot.

"'Who's the best hoopster in the school?'" Cricket read out loud. "'Find out at the contest.'"

"A basketball contest!" Leo said. "You know who'll win that."

"J.T." said Cricket. "Jason Tourville. No question."

"There's nobody in school who even comes close," said Leo. "Not even the big kids."

It was true that Jason was an amazing basket-ball player. Everybody knew it. They'd all seen him play every day at recess. He could sink a basket from over by the jungle gym! Nobody else at their school could do that.

At least that's what Cricket and Leo thought.

Molly knew different.

Why?

Because she could do it, too. Had done it. Many times. Only never (of course) when anybody from school was looking.

Molly's brothers were all really good at basketball. They had made sure she knew the basics by the time she was four. Now that she was ten, she could hold her own when they all played two-on-two in the driveway.

Molly wondered what Leo and Cricket — and everybody else in school — would think if they knew she could sink a free throw eight times out of ten. They'd be surprised, that was for sure!

But they'd never find out. Molly would never enter a contest like that, not in a million years. The idea of standing in the middle of the gym floor all by herself, while the whole school watched from the bleachers, made her dizzy.

Actually, it made her feel like throwing up. Molly glanced down the hall to the nurse's office, where she'd spent more than one afternoon with a stomachache. Usually that happened on days when oral reports were due. Mrs. Gleason was always really nice to Molly.

"Look at the prize!" Leo was saying meanwhile. "Good thing we have Jason."

Molly checked the poster as Cricket read out loud again.

"'The winner's class will receive the first of the new computers,'" Cricket read. "That's cool, I guess."

"Yeah, but look at what else we get," Leo said.

"'. . . and gets to pick out the pajamas that Mr. Connor will wear on Pajama Day!'" Cricket gave a little shriek and put a hand over her mouth. "Ha! That's great!"

Pajama Day was everybody's favorite day at school. Everybody but Molly's, that was. She always felt super self-conscious about coming to school in her nightgown. Last year she had actually stayed home, pretending to have a really bad sore throat. Still, she had to admit it would be fun to see the principal walking around all day wearing pajamas she had helped pick out.

"I hope we can find something really wild, like tie-dyed or with Bugs Bunny," Leo said. "Mr. Connor would look hilarious in that!"

He sounded so sure that their class was going to win. Molly thought he was probably right, with Jason as their not-so-secret weapon.

Disappointment

Jessie! Mr. Taylor's story was the first thing Molly thought about when she woke up the next morning. She pictured Jessie waking up in her room at the Rocking R Ranch. Would her father let her go on roundup this spring? Molly closed her eyes tight and wished really hard that he would. This cowboy stuff was kind of interesting, after all. Molly wanted to hear all about how they roped the calves and rounded up the cattle. If the story ended up being about a girl who did nothing but help her mother cook and sew, what fun would that be?

Molly dressed quickly and headed downstairs. She could hardly wait to get to school. The kitchen was full of the usual bustle of getting ready for school and work. Molly's dad skimmed the paper while he ate his toast. Her mom rummaged in her briefcase, looking for a report she'd misplaced. And her brothers sat around the table, shoving cereal into their mouths. Nobody ever talked much at breakfast.

"Shoot a few?" asked her brother Mark as they put their cereal bowls in the sink. "The bus isn't coming for ten minutes."

"Sure," said Molly. Mark was her favorite brother. He was only a year older. Stan and Matthew were both in middle school now, but Mark and Molly still rode the bus together.

Molly followed Mark out to the driveway. He grabbed their beat-up old basketball from the rack inside the garage and tossed it to her. "Let's play Horse," he said.

That was a game where the players took turns shooting baskets. Each player got to choose where to stand and what kind of shot to make. The next player had to copy that exact shot. If you missed a basket, you earned a letter. When you had enough letters to spell the word H-O-R-S-E, you were out.

The word *horse* made Molly think of Smokey,

Jessie's feisty little pinto pony. She smiled as she caught the ball. Its hard, pebbly texture felt so familiar in her hands. She adjusted her grip, glanced up at the basket, set herself, and let the ball fly. "Yes!" she yelled. She knew exactly how Jessie felt when she lassoed that fence post.

"Nice," said Mark as he retrieved the ball and took a shot himself. The ball bounced off the rim, and Molly ran for it. Mark was great at dribbling and passing, but he couldn't shoot nearly as well as Molly. Now he had an *H*.

"Make sure to set yourself before a shot like that," advised Molly's dad, who had come out of the house and was just getting into his car. "You'll have a better chance."

That's what Molly always told Mark. But she didn't say so now. Her dad didn't really talk about basketball with her. Just with her brothers. The guys watched games on TV together and sometimes even went to see a pro game. But Molly was never invited. She had the feeling her dad didn't think basketball was a sport for girls.

"Molly, your mom's inside cleaning up the

kitchen all by herself," he said now. "Does that seem fair?" He gave her a smile. "Maybe you could help her out."

Molly frowned. Dad never said things like that to any of her brothers. How fair did *that* seem? But *okay* was all Molly said. Her dad drove off, waving.

"Oh, well, you don't need the practice anyway," said Mark, noticing Molly's expression. "You're such a superstar. You're going to win that school-wide hoop shoot, aren't you?"

Molly stared at him. "What are you talking about?" she asked. "I'm not entering. No way!" How could Mark even think she would enter? Didn't he know her at all? Or was he just being mean, teasing her? That must be it.

Without another word, Molly tossed the ball to Mark, turned, and headed inside to help her mother.

She didn't talk to Mark at the bus stop, and when they got on the bus she walked right past the seat they usually shared.

Mark followed her. "Molliwog," he said quietly, so nobody would hear the special name he always called her. "I'm sorry. I didn't mean to tease you. Sometimes I just forget, that's all! You're not shy at home."

Molly shrugged. "No big deal," she said, looking at the back of the seat in front of her.

"I really am sorry," Mark repeated. "Anyway, you could win if you entered. You're definitely the best shooter in the school, even if nobody knows it."

"You really think so?" Molly asked. She turned to look at Mark.

"I know so," said her brother.

■ ■ ■

That morning, nobody in room 3B seemed to have a thing to share at sharing time. Even the chattiest kids were quiet. All they wanted was for Mr. Taylor to go on with the story. Finally, he stopped trying to coax news out of them. "Okay," he said. "Let's get on with Jessie's story."

"Yay!" shouted Cricket, right out loud.

Molly shouted the same thing — inside. She couldn't wait to hear what happened next.

They were already sitting around in the reading area since that was where they'd been having sharing time lately. So all Mr. Taylor had to do was reach up and turn on the lamp. It was as if the story had been right there waiting for them, all night. Mr. Taylor jumped right in.

■ ■ ■

It was still dark when Jessie woke up the next morning. But she didn't wake to the feeling of her pa shaking her shoulder. She woke to the sound of hooves and jingling spurs and shouts. The cowboys were gathering in the big dusty yard in front of the ranch house. Spring roundup was about to get underway.

Jessie jumped out of bed and ran to the window. Sure enough, there were about fifteen hands milling around on their horses, and Pa was off to the side, looking everything over. "Let's move out!" he finally cried. "Cookie, get that wagon going."

The chuck wagon always went on ahead of the crew, so the cook could set up a campsite and start dinner. Jessie watched out the window as the wagon rumbled on down the rutted track that led to the outer pastures. She swallowed hard. Disappointment tasted sour in her mouth.

"Jessie!" Pa shouted toward the house.

Her heart began to pound. Was he going to ask her along after all? Jessie pulled on trousers and a shirt, grabbed her hat, and reached for her lasso. Within minutes, she'd stumbled out onto the porch. A faint glow was just starting to light up the eastern sky. Soon the sun would be rising. Would Jessie and Smokey be riding with the others by the time its rays hit the ranch house?

But Pa just tipped his hat to her. "You be a good girl, now," he said solemnly. "Help your ma and do what she tells you, hear?"

Jessie felt tears spurt up into her eyes, but she held them back. "Yes, Pa. Good-bye, Pa," was all she could choke out. She stood there watching the boys and men ride off until the huge plume of dust they made had fallen slowly back to the dry brown yard.

Ma Has an Idea

Molly couldn't believe it. She almost felt like crying! How could Jessie's father be so mean?

"But she *has* to go!" said Jennifer, which was exactly what everybody else was thinking.

"The story's no fun if she just stays home," Jason said, agreeing for once with his twin.

"Well, the story isn't over yet, is it?" asked Mr. Taylor. "Should I go on?"

"Yes, yes, yes!" everybody yelled. They leaned forward, waiting to hear more.

■ ■ ■

Jessie felt her mother's arm around her shoulders. "It's never easy to watch them go, is it?" Ma said.

Jessie rubbed her nose. "Did you ever want to go with them?" she asked, leaning into her mother's warm hug. She knew that her mother loved to ride and that she was about as handy with a rope as anyone on the ranch. In the early days, before they had Jessie, Ma and Pa ran the ranch together. They both did whatever needed to be done, from taking care of sick cows to training wild mustangs to the harness. Back then, the ranch was a small operation, just a couple dozen head of cattle, and there had been no need for a spring roundup. But Ma had done everything else! Jessie had heard lots of stories about those times.

"Oh, maybe," Ma answered. "It does sound like fun sometimes. But they'll be back soon, and someone has to hold down the fort here at home. We can't have this place falling to pieces with everyone away, can we?"

She spoke lightly, but she gave Jessie's shoulder a squeeze, and Jessie knew that she understood. Then Ma guided Jessie back inside. "How about pie for breakfast?" she asked. "I saved you the last slice."

After she ate her pie, Jessie helped Ma wash

two sinkfuls of dishes. She felt grateful that Ma had let her sleep through breakfast. It would have been so sad to sit there watching all the hands shovel down their chow while Pa told them about the plans for roundup.

Once the kitchen was shipshape, Jessie went out to feed the chickens and milk Sadie, the cow, who they kept for milk, cream, and butter. Jessie turned Smokey out into the pasture, promising him a ride later in the day. He seemed a little lonely with all the other horses gone off to work the roundup. "I know you'd love to be out there with them," she told him, burying her face in his sweet-smelling neck. "So would I."

When she went back inside, Ma said it was time to catch up on mending. She must have seen Jessie's face fall — Jessie hated sewing more than any other chore — because she suggested they do their work on the porch. "Sun's up, and it's going to be a beautiful warm day," Ma said as she picked up her mending basket and led the way outside.

Jessie followed with an armload of shirts with

missing buttons, torn trousers, and socks with no heels. She sat down on the rocker next to her mother's and began to poke through the mending basket. "I'll thread some needles," she offered, knowing that her mother appreciated her sharp eyes and nimble fingers when it came to that task.

It was the one part of mending that Jessie didn't mind. When she was sewing or darning, she was always pricking her fingers. But she could thread five needles in no time, each with a different color. The best part was snipping off the thread with Ma's pretty golden scissors, the ones she'd brought all the way from Tennessee. They were beautiful, those scissors. Their pointy blades were as sharp as anything, and their handle was engraved with flowers and vines in a twining pattern.

■ ■ ■

The scissors! Molly felt her heart thump. Maybe now there was going to be some magic in her story. Sure, it was mostly a cowboy story, but it could still have magic in it, couldn't it? She leaned forward, listening closely.

■ ■ ■

Jessie and her mother sewed for hours, stopping only for a quick lunch at noontime. By afternoon, Jessie's fingers were cramped, and her head was aching. She was tired of squinting, tired of sharp needles sticking her thumb, tired of sitting still.

"Look who's here!" Ma said, shading her eyes to look across the yard. "Just in time. We're finished for the day."

It was Dexter, riding up on Red. "Afternoon, Miz Doyle," he said, touching the brim of his hat. "Hey, Jessie."

He slid off Red and looped the reins around a porch pillar. Then he plopped down into the chair next to Jessie's and heaved a big sigh.

"Is life really that hard, Dexter?" Jessie's mother asked with a little smile as she knotted the thread on the button she had attached.

"Well, it ain't — I mean, it isn't easy," Dexter answered. "Our cook, Wiz, can't find anyone to help him. Everybody who wants to work on a roundup is already hired on somewhere. We can't start roundup until he finds somebody, and Uncle Hank is champing at the bit."

Dexter's uncle Hank was running spring roundup that year since his father was back East visiting Dexter's ailing grandmother.

"Why don't you do it?" Jessie asked.

"I said I would," Dexter answered, "and Wiz said I'd be perfect. All he needs is an extra pair of hands. But Uncle Hank said he needs me in the saddle."

Jessie bit her lip. "I could do it," she blurted out suddenly. "But they'd never hire a girl."

Dexter shook his head. "You're sure right about that," he said. "Uncle Hank is even worse about that than your own pa."

Ma wasn't saying anything. But she looked thoughtful. Then, suddenly, she sat up straight. Her eyes were sparkling as she stared at Jessie. "You could do it," she said. "You've always wanted to go on roundup, and you should have your chance." She reached out to stroke Jessie's river of silky red hair. "Jessie," she said. "Hand me those scissors."

■ ■ ■

Now Molly's heart was really thumping. Was Jessie's mother going to do what Molly thought she might do? If she did, it would be the coolest thing ever.

This time, even Jennifer didn't interrupt. Nobody did. They all just waited, hardly daring to breathe. What would happen next?

Transformation

Snip, snip, snip, went the golden scissors. And long, shining locks of Jessie's hair began to fall to the rough boards of the porch floor.

Jessie's heart was thumping hard as she sat facing west toward the mountains. Her mother's sure, strong hands moved carefully around Jessie's head, which felt lighter by the minute.

Dexter was speechless, but his eyes were bright and his face was flushed pink. Jessie could tell he loved the idea as much as she did.

Finally, she was going to go on spring roundup — but she was going as a boy!

That is, if she could convince Wiz to hire her. If she could convince everybody that she was a boy.

"Lucky for me your pa's away!" Jessie said to Dexter as her mother finished up. "He might recognize me. Not that I've seen anybody in your family for ages. You always come over here. I haven't been to the Bar T since last Easter, I think."

"Nobody would recognize you anyway," Dexter said. "I mean, you look familiar, but so different, like you're your own cousin or something."

"That's it!" Ma said. "That's what you can tell them. Tell Wiz and Hank you're visiting from Montana, where you live on a ranch. You really do have cousins up that way, even though you've never met them."

"Ma!" Jessie said, whirling around with a smile on her face. "Are you telling me to lie?"

Ma blushed and put down the scissors. "I guess I am," she admitted. "But it's just a little fib. And it's for a good reason."

Jessie looked into her mother's face. "Won't you miss me?" she asked. "Won't you worry about me?"

"Both," said her mother, gathering her in for a big hug. "But I know you'll be safe with Dexter and his uncle, and I know how important this is to you. I'll make do."

"What if Pa finds out?" Jessie asked.

"He won't find out until roundup is over," Ma answered. "It'll be too late to do anything about it by then. And if I know your pa, he'll come around to understanding . . . after a while."

A long *while*, thought Jessie.

"Look at you!" Ma gazed at Jessie and shook her head. "You make a right good-looking boy."

Jessie shook her own head and felt nothing but the cool air on her neck. No hair sliding over her shoulders or brushing her cheek. Suddenly, it was easy to hold her head up high. It felt lighter than a feather. "I have to see," she said. She ran to the door and dashed inside to check her reflection in the mirror that hung in the parlor.

A slight, freckled boy stared back at her. A pale boy, with short red hair and brown eyes that looked much bigger than Jessie's. A boy dressed in the trousers and shirt Jessie had pulled on when she jumped out of bed that morning. For a moment, Jessie felt very strange. Her hair was the prettiest thing about her, and now it was gone. But that feeling passed as she grinned at herself in the mirror.

Dexter came up behind her. "What do you think?" he asked.

"I think I'm going on roundup!" And Jessie let out a cowboy whoop that shook every glass lamp in the parlor.

■ ■ ■

Everybody in room 3B whooped, too. Mr. Taylor grinned. "Happy now?" he asked, laughing.

Molly let out a breath. Yes, she was happy! Jessie was about to start on an incredible adventure, and they'd be hearing all about it.

Maybe those golden scissors really were magic, in a way. It was almost as if they'd given Jessie her wish, after all.

Jessie Gets a Job

Molly thought she was going to burst, waiting until the next day to find out what would happen to Jessie. But later that afternoon, Mr. Taylor surprised the class. "You've all gotten so much done today!" he said as they finished going over their spelling words. "How about if we get back to Jessie's story?"

Everybody jumped up and ran for the reading corner.

Mr. Taylor laughed. "I guess that's a yes," he said as he strolled over and turned on the lamp. He sat down, settled himself in his easy chair, and began.

● ● ●

"So, James, do you know how to cook?" Wiz asked, peering at Jessie intently.

Jessie wondered if this was a trick question. If

she said yes, would Wiz guess that James was actually a girl? "A — a little," she stammered, after a moment. Her head was still spinning. Only hours before, she'd been Jessie, sewing on the porch. Now she was James, asking Wiz for a job.

Wiz shrugged. "Doesn't really matter," he said. "As long as you can follow directions. I'll tell you what to do."

Jessie shot a look at Dexter. He waggled his eyebrows. She was in! "So, do I have the job?" she asked Wiz, just to make sure.

He nodded carelessly. "We head out first thing tomorrow," he said. "Wagon's already mostly stocked. We'll finish in the morning. Got your bedroll? You can sleep in the bunkhouse."

Jessie gave Dexter a wild look. She hadn't thought of that! How could she spend the night in a room full of rough, snoring cowboys? There was no privacy in a bunkhouse.

"Maybe James would rather stay with his horse," Dexter offered. "Just to settle him. Smokey can be a little high-strung in new places."

"Yes!" Jessie said with relief. "I'll just bed down in the barn."

Wiz shrugged. "Suit yourself," he said. "See you at breakfast. I won't need your help for that since we're still here at the ranch." He nodded brusquely and walked away.

Dexter grinned at Jessie. "You're coming!" he said. "This is going to be the best roundup ever."

Jessie smiled back a little uncertainly. What had she gotten herself into?

That night she hardly slept at all. She lay in a corner of Smokey's stall, listening to a barn full of restless horses. Jessie imagined that they felt the same mixture of excitement and nervousness that she did. They paced and snorted and kicked the walls of their stalls. Jessie took deep breaths of the warm, horse-smelling barn air and tried to calm herself. She must have finally fallen asleep because when she woke up the first thing she saw was Smokey, his white patches glowing in the early light.

He nudged her with his big nose as if to say,

"Time to get up!" When she got to her feet he nudged her again, looking for breakfast.

She fetched him some clean hay and stood watching for a moment as he chewed. "We're going on a big adventure," she told him, patting his neck.

Smokey tossed his head as he munched his hay. "I'm excited, too, but don't bother me while I'm eating," he seemed to be saying.

Jessie was rolling up her blankets when she heard the dinner bell ring. "Guess it's time for my breakfast!" she told Smokey.

The ranch house kitchen was crowded and steamy and smelled wonderfully of bacon and coffee. Dexter waved when Jessie came in, and he made room for her at the long table. None of the other cowboys even glanced up when she slipped into her seat. They were all too busy shoveling piles of food into their mouths.

"You'd think they weren't going to eat for weeks!" Jessie whispered.

"That's how they always eat," Dexter whispered back. "If you're looking for fancy table manners, you've picked the wrong group of friends."

But Jessie was used to watching cowboys eat. After all, she'd helped her mother feed plenty of hungry men.

"I got you a plateful," Dexter whispered, "so you wouldn't have to come face-to-face with my ma." He glanced over to the stove, where his mother was dishing out huge helpings of eggs, beans, and biscuits. "Not that she'd recognize you anyway. You sure do look different!"

"I feel different," said Jessie as she dug into her eggs. "I feel like a cowboy." Suddenly, she couldn't wait to get under way. She ate as fast as she could and then scraped back her chair and brought her plate to the sink, dodging Dexter's mother's eyes.

"I'm going to go help Wiz load the chuck wagon," she told Dexter. "See you out there!" Grabbing one last biscuit for the trail, she headed for the door.

"Hey, girl!" she heard someone shout behind her. "Where are you headed with that?"

Jessie froze. Had somebody guessed that James was not who he appeared to be?

■ ■ ■

Just then, the final bell rang.

"Oh, dear," said Mr. Taylor, looking up at the clock. "What a shame."

"But you can't stop now!" wailed Cricket.

"I have to," said Mr. Taylor. "Some of you have buses to catch. We'll pick up the story first thing tomorrow, I promise. Meanwhile, try not to worry too much about Jessie. And don't forget to do your math homework. Problems eight, nine, and ten at the end of chapter four."

Molly groaned. How in the world was she going to be able to pay attention to math when Jessie's whole life was in the balance? But Mr. Taylor was right. If she missed her bus, it was a long, long walk home. Her family lived way out at the end of State Road, where there were hardly any other houses. She gathered her things and headed outside. It felt strange to be in the school parking lot instead of in the dusty yard of the Double Bar T Ranch. She could just see it: the corral and the windmill and the cowboys on horseback, ready to head out on roundup.

She was sure that everything would work out

all right for Jessie. Wouldn't it? But she couldn't quite imagine how. If he discovered that she was a girl, Uncle Hank would never let her go along on roundup. Molly crossed her fingers, shut her eyes tight, and wished as hard as she could.

Molly's Secret

On the bus on the way home, Molly told Mark as much as she could remember about Jessie's story so far.

"I wish Ms. Marshall told stories like that," Mark said. "The only stories she ever tells are about her dumb old bird-watching vacation in Florida. Boring!"

Molly knew she was lucky to have Mr. Taylor for a teacher. She was already dreading next year when she'd probably have a regular teacher again, the kind who stuck to lesson plans and wouldn't have a clue how to tell wonderful stories. And to think she had been sort of scared of Mr. Taylor at first!

"Want to play?" Mark asked as they walked up the long dead-end road that led to their house.

"Play what?" Molly teased. "Monopoly? Video

games?" She knew perfectly well what Mark meant.

He made a face. "Duh. Basketball."

"Of course," she said happily. She always wanted to play. "But I'm going to do my math homework first, just so I can forget about it."

Molly's homework wasn't hard, and she and Mark were shooting baskets in the driveway by the time Stan and Matthew arrived home.

"Two-on-two?" Stan suggested.

"Only if I get Molly on my team," Mark said.

"Deal," said Matthew. "Prepare to get beaten. We'll even spot you five points."

"Don't bother," Molly said. "We can cream you without any help."

She wondered for a second what her classmates would think if they could hear her trash-talking that way. It was something she and her brothers did all the time. But it was so different from the way she acted in class.

Molly rolled up her sleeves and flipped her braids out of the way. "Let's go!" she said, tossing the ball to Matthew. He was standing over by the petunias, which counted as out of bounds. He tossed it inbounds to Stan, and the game was under way.

Stan dribbled toward the basket, faking first to the right and then to the left. But Molly was all over him. She knew every one of her brother's moves. He couldn't get a shot no matter how hard he tried. Finally, he pivoted and passed the ball to Matthew.

Mark tried to guard Matt, but that was never easy. Matthew was the tallest brother, and he could jump higher than any of them. He brushed off Mark like his little brother was a bothersome gnat. The ball sailed through the air and swooshed through the basket. "Nothing but net!" Matthew crowed.

Molly grabbed the rebound and flipped it to Mark, who had already moved out of bounds. He tossed the ball to put it back in play. Molly could feel Matthew coming up behind her. He probably figured she was going to move to her favorite shooting spot, beneath the basket. But she fooled him. After faking a move to her left, she stepped back and took a long shot over Matthew's head, letting the ball fly — out, out, out like Jessie's lasso — in a long, high arc.

"Yes!" she shouted, pumping her fist as the ball dropped through the basket. "That's three points!" Molly loved making shots like that.

"Molly?"

Molly whirled around. Who was calling her name? The voice was familiar. "Leo!" she said when she spotted her classmate standing at the end of the driveway. He had his little spotted dog, Tracker, with him, on the end of a long red leash. Leo was staring at Molly. His mouth was hanging open. "What are you doing here?" Molly asked. She felt the familiar heat creep into her face.

"What am *I* doing?" Leo said. "What are *you* doing? Since when do you play basketball?"

Molly looked down at the driveway. She couldn't speak. What was she supposed to say anyway?

"She's played since she was about this high," Matthew said, holding a hand out at waist height. "So what? Why shouldn't she?"

"Who are you?" Stan asked. He stood with the

ball cradled in the crook of his elbow, giving Leo a challenging look.

"I — I'm Leo. From school." He looked down at his dog. "Tracker ran off and I had to look all over for her. I just found her in that park on Martin Street."

Molly remembered the time Tracker had run away for days. She had never seen Leo so upset. She was glad Leo had found his dog quickly this time, but now she just wanted him to go away.

Leo just stood there. He was still staring at Molly. "Really, Molly, it's cool! You're good, too. I saw you make that basket."

Molly blushed harder. She didn't know where to look.

"She's awesome," Mark said. "She's probably better than that kid in your class."

"Jason Tourville," Leo said. He gave Molly an appraising look. "Yeah, she might even be better than Jason," he said thoughtfully.

Molly held her breath and hoped that he wouldn't say it.

But he did.

"You should enter the contest," Leo said. "Then our class would definitely win."

"No," Molly said quietly.

"Why not?" Leo asked.

Molly just shook her head. Her knees were feeling all watery just thinking about it.

"Because she doesn't want to," Matthew said.

"And she doesn't have to," said Stan. Both of them knew all about the contest by now, but they hadn't even suggested that Molly take part in it. They knew better.

"And if you keep bugging her about it —" Mark said, taking a step toward Leo.

Leo held up his hands. "Okay, okay," he said.

Mark gave Molly a quick look. Then he turned back to Leo. "In fact," he said, "I think Molly would be happier if you didn't tell anybody in school about this."

Molly nodded. Mark was absolutely right. She couldn't stand it if everybody found out and made a fuss about it.

"Well —" Leo began.

Mark took another step toward him.

"Okay!" Leo said. "Fine. But I don't get it. What's the big deal?"

"No big deal," Stan said. "Just keep it quiet."

"Bye-bye, now," Matthew said.

Leo took the hint. "Let's go, Tracker," he said. He and his dog headed off without another word.

Molly watched him go. Then she turned to Mark. "Thanks," she whispered. She knew that none of her brothers would really have started a fight with Leo. They were just pretending to be threatening. But it had worked. Leo had left.

Mark shrugged. "In a way, he's right," he said gently. "You *would* probably win, and your class would get to choose Mr. Connor's PJs. Everybody would think you were cool."

Molly nodded and tried to swallow past the big lump in her throat. Why did she have to be so shy? Of course it would be fun to have all her classmates know she was a good basketball player. Of course it would be fun to win the contest for Mr. Taylor's class. But there was just no way. And she was glad her brothers understood.

The Magic Kettle

Molly was nervous about seeing Leo the next morning in class. In fact, she was dreading it. But it turned out to be just fine. And she shouldn't have been so surprised. After all, Leo wasn't a jerk. He was a really nice guy. When she came into room 3B, Leo was already at his desk. He glanced up at her, gave her a little secret smile, and pretended to zip his lip.

"Thanks," she mouthed. She knew she was blushing, but that was okay. Now she could concentrate on the important thing: Jessie's story. She remembered that when Mr. Taylor left off the day before, somebody was calling out to Jessie as if they knew she was a girl! That would mess up everything. What was it the cowboy had said? "Hey, girl, where are you headed with that?"

Jennifer seemed worried, too. "Does someone know Jessie is a girl?" she asked once the class was settled in the reading corner after sharing time, ready for Mr. Taylor to pick up the story.

"Let's find out," he answered, reaching up to turn on the lamp. Then he picked up right where he had left off, with the cowboy calling out to Jessie as she was about to head out the ranch house door with a biscuit in her hand.

■ ■ ■

"Hey, girl!" she heard someone shout behind her. "Where are you headed with that?"

Jessie froze. Had somebody guessed that James was not who "he" appeared to be? "Keep moving, silly," Dexter whispered, poking her in the back. "It's just one of the cowboys talking to our dog. She stole his piece of bacon."

Jessie started walking toward the door again, her heart beating like an Indian tom-tom. Posing as a boy was nerve-racking! How was she going to make it through roundup?

A few minutes later, Jessie let out a loud "Oof!" as she helped Wiz heave a barrel of flour into the chuck box, the storage space in the back of the chuck wagon.

"That's the last of it," Wiz said, dusting off his hands as he looked with satisfaction at the neatly packed supplies. Two weeks' worth of food, plus all the pots, pans, spoons, dishes, and utensils needed for cooking and eating it, all tucked neatly into the wagon's nooks and crannies and cubbyholes. Everything was made out of tin so it wouldn't break as the wagon trundled along. Everything except the sourdough crock, that is. The big pottery jug held a mixture of flour, water, and yeast, and it was always kept filled so that Wiz could quickly produce biscuits for every meal.

There were medical supplies, too: cloth bandages and soap, needles and thread for sewing up cuts, splints for broken arms or legs. Every cook on the range had to know more than just how to cook a pot of beans. Usually the cook was as close to a real doctor as any hurt or sick cowboy was going to see.

Not only that, he had to know how to drive oxen, butcher a steer for dinner, ride a horse well enough to help when he was needed, and tell a good joke or sing a tuneful song as part of the nightly campfire entertainment.

While Jessie and Wiz were loading, there had been a steady stream of cowboys coming by to stow their bedrolls in the front of the chuck wagon. Wiz had introduced James to the men. "That's Pinky," he'd said, "and that there is Fats." Jessie tried to keep track, but there were too many new faces. Luckily for her, a lot of the nicknames told you exactly what the cowboy looked like.

Most times, anyway.

"Did you meet Tiny yet?" Dexter whispered, coming up behind Jessie. He tossed his bedroll into the wagon, then nodded at an enormously tall, wide man.

Jessie stifled a giggle. Of course they called him Tiny.

"Ready to head out?" Wiz called just then as he hauled himself up to the driver's seat of the chuck wagon. "Going to tie your horse to the wagon and travel with me?"

Jessie shook her head. "Thanks, but I'd rather

ride this morning," she said politely. Smokey was saddled and ready to go. In fact, he was raring to go. He'd been pawing at the ground for at least half an hour.

With Dexter giving her a leg up, Jessie swung onto Smokey's broad back and sat there for a second. The sun was just rising, and the eastern sky was painted with pink and gold and decorated with tattered rags of white clouds. Jessie took a deep breath. She thought of her ma, who was probably tossing feed to the chickens right now. She thought of her pa, probably just stretching his stiff body after a rough night's sleep on hard ground. She felt as if she were leaving for a long journey, even though she'd probably never be more than ten or fifteen miles away.

"See you at lunchtime, James!" Dexter called.

Jessie touched her fingers to the brim of her hat in a cowboy salute. "We'll have some grub waiting!" she promised. "Giddyap," she told Smokey, giving him a soft kick in the flanks. And Jessie was off, on her first roundup ever.

It was chilly that morning, and after half an hour

Jessie could still see her breath and Smokey's as they moseyed along behind the chuck wagon. The air was fresh and clean, the sky was crystal blue, and the sun was all the way up by then, shining for all it was worth. Everything Jessie looked at seemed to sparkle.

Smokey kept trying to break into a trot, but Jessie held him back. "Behave yourself!" she scolded him laughingly. "It's going to be a long couple of weeks," she added. "Better take it easy and save your energy for when you really need it." Jessie imagined that she and Smokey might get invited to help when branding started. Or there might be a stampede, and all hands would have to jump into action. Not that she hoped for a stampede.

A stampede was one of the worst things that could happen on a roundup or cattle drive. Jessie had heard her father tell terrible tales about cattle spooked by snakes, or loud noises, or even a shirt flapping in the wind. A herd of frightened cattle would not stop running. The huge, panicked beasts would trample everything in their path, including any cowboy unlucky enough to fall off his horse in the confusion. Sometimes the cattle would even run off a cliff or into a river, and dozens of them would be killed. No rancher could afford that kind of loss.

Jessie rode contentedly all morning, her thoughts drifting as she watched the scenery slide by from high on Smokey's back. She stayed far enough behind the chuck wagon to avoid the dust cloud it kicked up, but near enough to make sure she didn't lose sight of it. It wouldn't do to get lost on her first day of work.

Finally, she saw the chuck wagon stop. By the time she had caught up to it, Wiz had tied up the oxen. Next he pulled down the door of the chuck box and propped it up on its folding leg, forming their kitchen table.

"Nice ride?" he asked as Jessie slipped down off Smokey's back.

She grinned and nodded. "How will everybody find us?"

"Oh, they'll find us," Wiz assured her. "Cowboys always find their way to grub. Ready to work?" he asked.

Jessie nodded again.

Wiz started pulling things out of the chuck box: onions, flour, and beans that had been soaking in his huge round black kettle. He held up a big sharp knife and a bag of onions. "Start chopping," he said. "I'll get the fire started."

Jessie hesitated. Chopping onions was the one job she couldn't stand. It always made her cry.

Wiz raised an eyebrow.

Jessie knew she couldn't afford to make him mad. She'd been lucky to get this job. She held out her hand for the knife.

Soon the first cowboys began to arrive, hungry and ready for lunch. Jessie was tired by then; cooking for cowboys was hard work! But she pulled a ladle out of the chuck box and got ready to serve the delicious-smelling chili she'd helped to make.

"What do you have in your magic kettle today?" Tiny asked Wiz as he clambered off his horse and peered into the big black kettle, which was now bubbling away over a fire pit. The kettle hung from an iron bar resting across two uprights that Jessie had helped pound into the earth.

"Magic kettle?" Jessie asked.

"That's what we call it," Tiny told her. "This man is a wizard. Best cook in five states. I've seen him make a first-rate meal out of a handful of wrinkled old beans and some stew meat not fit for a dog."

■ ■ ■

Molly couldn't believe it. Her magic kettle was nothing but a cook pot! That didn't seem fair at all. She'd wanted the kind of kettle that makes enchanted soup that turns people invisible, or the kind that grants wishes. Not the kind that holds chili, no matter how good the chili happened to be.

But what could she do? She was beginning to realize that Mr. Taylor's stories didn't always turn out the way you wanted them to — but they always turned out great.

She even had to admit that she kind of liked how Wiz had gotten his nickname, from being a wizard at cooking.

■ ■ ■

"So that's where you got your name," Jessie said. Wiz nodded, looking a little embarrassed.

"It's not like my grub is anything fancy," he muttered.

"Who needs fancy?" Tiny roared. "I just want a full belly. And no bellyache afterward."

Jessie laughed.

"Can't afford a bellyache with the Lost Gulch Gang around," the cowboy named Pinky said. "We're going to have to be on our guard, from what I hear."

Jessie's heart beat a little faster. "The Lost Gulch Gang?" she asked. She'd heard that name before.

"Rustlers," Dexter said, slipping off Red and tying him to the chuck wagon.

Jessie knew all about rustlers from her father. They were criminals who roamed the range, stealing calves and putting their own brands on them, or changing the brands on grown cattle by adding a loop to make a *P* into a *B*, or a *C* into an *O*.

"We ran into the boys from the Lazy S a few miles back, and they told us to keep our eyes peeled. They've already had ten calves stolen!"

Jessie had been to the Lazy S Ranch. She knew their cowboys used the same range, so they were out on roundup, too. They must really be upset to lose all those calves. A few thefts like that could undo a whole year's worth of ranch work.

"I guess these rustlers are pretty nasty characters," Dexter finished. "I hope they get caught soon." He accepted a plate of chili from Jessie. "Thanks, Jess."

Jessie frowned at him.

"I mean, James," Dexter said quickly, looking around to see if anyone had heard.

Wiz was standing nearby, and Jessie could have sworn that he gave her a curious look. But he didn't say a word. He just pulled another pan of biscuits off the fire and began to hand them out.

■ ■ ■

"Dexter better be more careful!" said Cricket just as the bell rang.

Mr. Taylor nodded. "I suppose he should," he said. "Well, I think that's it for today. We still have a lot to do. We'll pick up the story tomorrow."

Everybody groaned. Tomorrow seemed a long way off! But it turned out they didn't have to wait that long, after all.

Rustlers!

After lunch that day, everybody in Molly's class charged out to the playground, the way they always did. Usually they all played kickball, teaming up against Ms. Baker's class. But these days everybody wanted to practice for the Hoop Shoot. Almost every kid on the playground lined up and took turns shooting baskets, trying all kinds of different techniques.

Molly hung back and watched while she pretended to read her book. She was in her usual spot, on the swinging rope bridge near the top of the jungle gym. Sometimes Molly played kickball or joined a group of girls on the swings, but she felt most comfortable being off by herself. Anyway, she really did want to read her book. It was *Half Magic*, about some brothers and sisters who get their wishes made half true. It was funny and exciting, but somehow it wasn't holding Molly's interest that day. She kept sneaking peeks at the kids who were trying to make baskets.

Trying was the word. Not too many balls swished through the net. There were a lot of near misses and a lot of far misses, like when Oliver tried his special over-the-shoulder-with-eyes-closed shots. The only person who got the ball into the basket almost every time was Jason.

He kept trying longer and longer shots, showing off a little, Molly thought. He shot from near the swings, then from the base of the jungle gym beneath Molly's perch, then from over by the slide.

"Hey, watch this!" he yelled the next time his turn came up. Holding the ball in the crook of his arm, he climbed up the ladder to the slide. Standing at the top, he turned toward the basket and took aim.

"Jason Tourville!" yelled Ms. Woods, the playground supervisor. "What do you think you're doing! Come down from there."

Jason did come down.

But he didn't come down the slide or climb down the ladder.

He fell.

Molly saw it all. Jason lost his balance, grabbed the ball instead of the railing, and flew right off the slide, landing with a thump on the ground.

"Jason!" yelled Jennifer. She ran over to her brother. "Are you okay?"

Suddenly, Jason was surrounded by people. Ms. Woods was helping him up off the ground.

Molly felt frozen in place and a little sick. Was Jason badly hurt? His face looked white, and he was holding his right arm in a funny way. She could hear him moaning all the way from where she was sitting.

Ms. Woods called the office on her walkie-talkie and told them what had happened. Then she walked Jason inside to see the nurse.

By the time recess was over, Jason's mom had picked him up.

Back in room 3B, everybody was talking about it. "I heard they're going straight to the emergency room," said Cricket. "I think his arm bone was, like, sticking out!"

"Jennifer got to go with him," Leo reported. "She looked really upset."

"So did his mom," said Oliver.

"She should be used to it by now," said Cricket. "Jason's always hurting himself. Remember last year when he cracked his head on the sidewalk?"

Finally, Mr. Taylor had to whistle to get everyone's attention. "I can see you won't be able to concentrate on anything else today," he said. "So instead of working on math, why don't we go on with Jessie's story?"

"But what about Jason and Jennifer?" asked Cricket.

"They'll catch up," Mr. Taylor promised. "I'll make sure of that." He led the way over to the reading corner and turned on the lamp while everybody settled in. Then he started the story again.

■ ■ ■

"What? Oh!" Jessie's head jerked up and she realized she had been dozing off again. She was

sitting on the wagon seat next to Wiz as they jogged along to that night's campsite. She'd been so tired after cooking and serving lunch that she had decided to tie Smokey to the back of the chuck wagon and keep Wiz company for a while. But the combination of the strong springtime sun, the hard work, and the excitement of the past few days was too much for Jessie. She couldn't keep her eyes open!

"That's all right," Wiz said. "Go ahead. You'll need all the sleep you can grab." He flicked his whip at the oxen. "Get up, Sal. Get up, Jack. I think these beasts are practically asleep, too!"

Jessie dozed off and on until the wagon stopped for the night. Then it was time to work.

She helped make a fire, chopped more onions, rolled out some biscuits, stirred the magic kettle, and washed up the cooking things with water drawn from the big barrel they'd filled back at the ranch.

She and Wiz had just barely gotten their work done when the first cowboys showed up in camp, driving a small herd of cattle in front of them.

"Eight calves in this bunch!" said Tiny as he rode up on his horse. "That's a good start!"

"If we can hang on to them all." As usual, Uncle Hank was frowning. "We'll keep the cattle in Chico's Canyon tonight. They'll be safe there, but with those rustlers in the neighborhood we're going to have to start all-night watches. If the gang shows up, the watchman can fire three gunshots. The rest of us will ride right out to help fight them off."

Rusty groaned. "Guess I'll go first," he said.

The men and boys unsaddled their horses, all except for Rusty. He began to herd the cattle toward the nearby canyon. As it grew dark, he would sing softly to the cattle to keep them calm. Jessie loved all those sweet, mournful cowboy songs.

"Smells good." Dexter nodded at the magic kettle and gave Jessie a wink. He and the other cowboys grabbed their bedrolls off the wagon and laid them out near the cook fire.

Soon everyone was sitting around the campfire, digging into the chili Jessie and Wiz had ladled out.

There wasn't much talk except for the occasional, "Great grub, Wiz!" or a request for more biscuits. The cowboys were hungry after a hard day's work, and their attention was on the food.

Afterward, while Jessie helped Wiz clean up, the hands leaned back on their bedrolls and began to swap stories and sing songs. The sun had already gone down over the mountains, and now the sky deepened from robin's-egg blue to violet. High, wispy white clouds began to fill the sky. Mare's tails, Slim called them. "Means the weather's about to change," he would say, looking up at the sky. A huge, silvery moon, almost full, began to peek over the horizon.

Jessie watched for the first star to make a wish on, but the clouds had moved in and there wasn't a twinkle to be found.

■ ■ ■

Molly caught her breath. She had asked for a wishing star. Why did it have to be cloudy? But she didn't say a thing. She didn't want Mr. Taylor to stop the story for even a second. And surely a star would show up eventually.

"*I hope I get to do more than just chop onions* and wash pots on this roundup," Jessie said under her breath, in case one of the unseen stars could hear her.

"Bet I can guess what you're wishing for," Dexter said, coming up behind her.

Jessie thought he probably could. Dexter knew her pretty well after all these years.

"I'm heading out to relieve Rusty soon," said Dexter. "Uncle Hank says I'm old enough to handle the first night shift. He figures the rustlers will strike closer to dawn, if at all. Want to keep me company while I'm on watch?"

"Sure," said Jessie. "I'll be done here in a few minutes. If Wiz says I can go, I'll saddle up Smokey."

A little while later, Dexter and Jessie rode away from the campfire, into the velvety darkness. Suddenly, Jessie felt very small, out there in the middle of the range. She pictured her ma, back home in the cozy lamplit parlor. She was surely either sewing or reading. And here was Jessie, jogging along on Smokey through the deep, dark night.

At first, Jessie's heart was thumping away. The night was too dark, too quiet away from the campfire. She imagined the Lost Gulch Gang, criminals with steely eyes, springing up out of the shadows. She'd never seen a rustler, but she could imagine they might look pretty scary.

By the time they arrived at Chico's Canyon, Jessie felt better. She'd been here before; she had played cowboys and Indians with Dexter in the canyon on more than one sunny winter day. The canyon had a narrow entrance, barely wide enough for one horse and rider to walk through. Then it opened out into a wide, open space surrounded by high, red-streaked clay cliffs. Nobody could get in or out except by the entrance, which was why it was a perfect place to corral and watch over the herd of cattle.

"Save me any grub?" Rusty asked when they rode into the canyon and told him they were there to relieve him.

"There's a plate waiting for you by the fire,"

Jessie assured him. "Wiz is guarding it with his life."

As she and Dexter began riding long, slow circles around the cattle, Jessie relaxed. The herd was calm tonight. She could hear their contented sighs and a grunt as one lay down, or a munching noise as another grazed on the long grass that covered the canyon floor.

Jessie could tell that Dexter was enjoying the quiet night, too. They didn't talk much as they rode side by side around the herd. On their fourth or fifth trip around, Dexter began to sing, and Jessie joined in. They worked their way into "Oh, Susannah" and were halfway into "My Darling Clementine" when Jessie spotted a figure on horseback slipping through the canyon entrance. *That can't be Tiny,* she thought in the middle of a verse. *He's not due to relieve us for another hour.* She kept singing, but suddenly her voice began to sound quavery.

If it wasn't Tiny, who was it? And why wasn't he saying anything?

Jessie's voice faltered. She stopped singing.

So did Dexter.

"Who — who's there?" he called.

The figure on horseback didn't answer.

Jessie knew why.

It had to be one of the Lost Gulch Gang.

The Star

The figure rode closer. Jessie held her breath. Smokey seemed to sense her nervousness. He snorted and tossed his head.

"Who's there?" Dexter asked again. Jessie could tell he was as scared as she was.

"I'll ask you the same," said the man, riding up so close that their horses practically touched noses.

He was tall. Jessie could tell that even though the man was on horseback. He wore a dark cowboy hat that shaded his face so that Jessie couldn't see his eyes, even in the bright moonlight. But he flipped open his vest and Jessie saw the unmistakable glint of a shining metal star. "Sheriff Gates," he said. "Out looking for rustlers. Have I found a couple?"

■ ■ ■

Molly drew in a breath. "That's not the kind of star I meant!" she said. She hadn't meant to say it out loud. When Mr. Taylor looked at her, she shut her mouth, blushing.

"Well, it's the kind of star that's in the story," Mr. Taylor said with a little smile. "Should I go on, or not?"

Molly was too embarrassed to speak. She just nodded, and Mr. Taylor seemed to know what that meant. He went on with the story.

■ ■ ■

The sheriff wore a serious look, but Jessie could tell that he was joking about them being rustlers. He obviously knew that they were just a couple of youngsters pulling watch duty, just like they could tell right off that he was a real sheriff and not a rustler pretending to be a lawman. But she and Dexter spoke up quickly, just in case there was any misunderstanding.

"Dexter Lawrence, Double Bar T Ranch," Dexter said in a firm voice.

Jessie tried to echo his tone. "Jessie —" she began. "James!" she corrected herself.

"Jessie James, eh?" asked the sheriff. "I knew I'd find a desperado in here." He grinned, and Jessie knew right away that she liked him.

"Are you two youngsters the only ones here?"

Dexter nodded. "We're on watch," he said.

"For the Lost Gulch Gang, I presume?"

Dexter nodded again.

"Well, you may see them sooner than you thought," said Sheriff Gates. "I heard tell from an informant that they're on their way here." He squinted up at the moon, which was still shrouded by clouds. By now it was almost directly overhead. "My posse's on its way, but I have a feeling the gang will get here first. Is there anyone else around to help?"

Dexter nodded. "Back at camp," he said. "If you fire your gun three times, they'll come running."

"If I fire my gun, the gang will know I'm here, and they'll run off before I can catch them." He thought for a moment. Then he squinted at Jessie and Dexter. "Mind if I deputize you?"

Jessie gulped. "Deputize?"

"I need your help," the sheriff explained. "I want

to trap those rascals now, before they cause any more trouble."

"But what can we do?" Jessie tried to keep her voice from squeaking.

The sheriff thought for a moment, pushing his hat back and scratching his head. Then he spoke. "Stand guard just outside the mouth of the canyon. Give an owl hoot when you hear them coming. They'll ride right in here, hoping to make off with your calves. But I'll be waiting."

He put his hand on his hip, and Jessie saw the glint of a silver pistol.

"When you hear me tell them to put their hands up, get ready! They may try to bolt."

"But —" Dexter began.

"No time for more planning," Sheriff Gates interrupted. "They'll be here any minute." He wheeled his horse around and began to ride deeper into the shadowed canyon. "Hide yourselves well out there!" he called. "I want them to think the place is unguarded."

"Yikes," Jessie said under her breath.

"Yikes is right," Dexter said. "What'll we do?"

"We'll do what he told us to do," Jessie said. "It's an adventure!" Suddenly, she was excited. She and Dexter were going to help trap the rustlers! "Come on, Smokey," she said. She steered him toward the canyon wall. Slipping off his back, she tied him to a piñon tree. "You stay in here and be a good boy," she said, giving him a precious carrot that she'd taken from Wiz's supplies. She rubbed his nose and kissed his big, flat cheek.

Dexter tied Red up next to Smokey. Then he and Jessie headed for the mouth of the canyon.

"I'll hide on this side, in these mesquite bushes," Jessie whispered. "You hide over there, behind that boulder."

"When did you get so bossy?" Dexter hissed, but he did as he was told.

Jessie hunkered down behind the scratchy, spicy-smelling shrub. Her heart was beating fast. She reached down and touched the lasso hanging from her belt, just for good luck.

The bright moon shone down, casting long

shadows. Jessie peeked across the way to where Dexter was hiding, but she couldn't see him at all. Good. She sat quietly, listening to the still night.

"Hear anything?" Dexter called in a hoarse whisper.

"Shh!" said Jessie. She *had* just heard something. A distant thumping, a jingling of spurs. "They're coming!" she said.

Sure enough, a few minutes later three horsemen appeared out of the dark. Jessie's newfound courage fled when she saw them, three dark figures with dark deeds on their minds. She felt paralyzed, frozen in place.

Just as well, she told herself. *If I move, they might see me.*

The three men did not seem to notice a thing as they rode brazenly toward the canyon entrance. One was tall in the saddle, one slumped lazily, and the third wore the jingly spurs. All three wore bandannas over their noses and mouths. Most cowboys did that to keep dust out of their lungs. These three men did it so nobody could see their faces.

"In here," Jessie heard one of them say. "I knew

they'd use this canyon. Probably only one man on watch, too. This'll be like taking candy from a baby."

Hah! Jessie thought to herself. *Little did they know.* She wished Dexter was hiding right next to her so she could elbow him in the ribs.

She held her breath as the men rode by. As soon as they'd passed her, she made a noise like the owl who lived in the barn back home: "*Who-who!*" she hooted, a little shakily. Then she held her breath again as she waited to hear Sheriff Gates surprise the three men.

She was just about to keel over from lack of air when she heard a gunshot split the quiet night. "Hold it right there!" yelled the sheriff. "Hands up! You're surrounded."

Jessie wondered if the sheriff's ruse would work. The clouds had parted, and the moon was so bright that the rustlers could probably see as clear as day that there was only one man facing them. She looked toward the east, hoping against hope that the sheriff's posse would arrive in time. But the horizon was empty in the moonlight.

Then Jessie heard hoofbeats — from inside the canyon. They were heading straight for the canyon opening! "Let's get out of here!" she heard someone shout. The Lost Gulch Gang was about to make a getaway. The first horseman made a break for it.

Across the way, Dexter leaped to his feet and, quick as a wink, threw his lasso. It looped out easily and landed perfectly around the rider's shoulders. Dexter yanked it tight, and the man flew backward off his horse, landing on the ground.

"Got him!" Dexter crowed.

But another rider was right behind the first, and there was no way Dexter could recover his lasso in time to throw it again. The hoofbeats grew closer.

Jessie touched her own lasso. Then she grabbed it and held it tight. She glanced across to the other side of the canyon's mouth and spotted a sturdy stump, about waist-high. Would it work? Jessie knew she couldn't hesitate. Taking a deep breath, she raised her lasso and sent it spinning toward the stump. The circle at the end of her rope drifted out, out, out and fell gently onto its target. Jessie pulled on the rope with all her strength, digging in her heels as the outlaw's horse approached.

The rope was taut and all but invisible in the night. But would the horse sense it? Jessie didn't have long to wonder.

The horse and rider burst out of the canyon's opening seconds later. Jessie leaned her whole weight against the rope. And yes! The horse saw the rope and stopped short. The animal didn't fall, but its rider flew right off its back! The tall man hit the ground with a thump. He cursed loudly as his horse, regaining its balance, galloped off into the night.

Moments later, Sheriff Gates rode out of the canyon with another horse walking meekly behind his. On its back was the third outlaw, his hands securely tied behind him.

"Excellent work!" said the sheriff. He hopped down off his horse to tie up the other two outlaws who lay stunned and groaning on the ground. "Thanks to you two, these three have rustled their last cows." Solemnly, he shook Dexter's hand. Then he shook Jessie's. "You're one spunky gal," he said to her with a wink.

Jessie gulped. How did he know she was really a girl? She wasn't sure what to do. Should she deny it and insist that she was a boy? It probably wouldn't do any good.

She was saved by the sound of hoofbeats. "Your posse!" she said, turning to look at the group of five riders pulling their horses up near the canyon's mouth. Good. Now the sheriff would have help bringing the Lost Gulch Gang into town, where an empty jail cell sat waiting.

Molly on the Spot

That afternoon, Molly's head was so full of Jessie's story that she could not seem to concentrate on basketball. She felt bad that Jason and Jennifer had missed such an exciting part.

"What is up with you?" Mark asked when she missed her third try at a shot from the top of the key. "You *always* make that shot."

Molly just shrugged. She was thinking about rustlers and lassos and pounding hoofbeats. But as soon as she got the ball, she tried the shot again. It bothered her to miss it.

"Hey, there's that kid again!" Stan said as he caught the rebound that sprang off the rim.

Molly followed his glance to the end of the driveway. Leo was standing there, Tracker at his side on the same red leash.

"What, did you lose your dog again?" Matthew asked.

Leo shook his head. "I came to talk to Molly."

Molly didn't want to talk to Leo. Right at that moment, all she wanted was to make that shot.

She bounced the ball once, twice, three times. She held it in her hands. She spun it. Bounced it one more time. Then she looked up at the basket, took careful aim, and let the ball fly.

Swish!

It dropped through the net. Molly let out a sigh of relief as her brothers lined up for high fives.

Leo stepped forward. "That's what I wanted to talk to you about," he said.

"No," said Molly. She knew exactly what he was going to say.

Leo didn't seem to hear her. "See, it turns out that Jason did break his wrist, and . . ."

"No," repeated Molly.

"Please?" Leo pleaded. "We need you. Mr. Taylor's class has to go down in history for picking the wildest pajamas ever for Mr. Connor."

Molly just shook her head.

"Is this about that contest?" Stan asked.

"The Hoop Shoot!" Matthew said. "Molly, maybe Leo's right. Your class *does* need you. You could win that thing in a minute."

Molly turned to him, frowning. How could he? He knew she would never do anything like that.

Then Mark spoke up. "Think about it, Molly," he said quietly. "Wouldn't it be kind of cool to show everybody what you can do?"

Molly looked at him.

"We'd all be there," he said.

Molly pictured the scene. A gym full of people, everyone's eyes on her. Molly. The shy girl.

Then she thought about Jessie and how brave she was. Jessie was out there catching rustlers! And she had to pretend to be a boy to go on roundup. Nowadays, girls could be in the Hoop Shoot just like boys could. Maybe Molly owed it to Jessie to try. What was the big deal? A stupid Hoop Shoot. It was nothing compared to what Jessie had done. And she knew Mr. Taylor would be so proud of her if she even entered, much less won.

She took a deep breath.

"Okay," she said. "I'll do it."

■ ■ ■

The next morning, Leo kept his promise and made it all the way through sharing time without mentioning Molly's promise. Molly had a feeling that Mr. Taylor noticed that something was up, but he didn't say a word. He just welcomed Jason and Jennifer back — and encouraged Jason to tell about his trip to the emergency room.

After everybody had signed Jason's neon-yellow cast, Mr. Taylor suggested that it was time to catch up with Jessie. He led the way over to the reading corner, turned on the lamp, and went back to the story.

■ ■ ■

"Know how to tell when the coffee's ready?" Wiz asked a sleepy Jessie. The sun wasn't even up yet. The whole world was in shades of gray, but it was time to get breakfast started, so Jessie and Wiz were up and moving around.

"When it smells right?" Jessie guessed.

Wiz smiled. "Nope! We drop a horseshoe in there. When it floats, the coffee's done." He let out a long, low chuckle when he saw Jessie's face. "I'm joking," he said. "It's an old cowboy saying. These boys like their coffee strong, but not that strong." He hooked the big blue enamel coffeepot off the cook fire. "I'd say it's ready now," he said. "Better be. I see some of the hands stirring."

Rusty and Tiny were both already on their feet, rolling up their bedrolls. Tiny rubbed his back and groaned. "You sure can spend the night fast with this outfit," he said. "Seems like I only lay down about five minutes ago."

Wiz rang the iron triangle. "Come and get it, or I'll throw it in the creek!" he hollered.

Jessie knew there wasn't a creek in sight, but the old joke did the trick. The cowboys stretched and got up, rubbing their eyes. Some came over to the chuck wagon to splash water on their faces. Others went to check on their horses. Before long, the sun was up and all the hands were sitting around the fire, drinking strong black coffee and eating biscuits and gravy.

Jessie was at the fire pouring more coffee for Pinky when she saw Sheriff Gates ride up. He touched his hat in a quick salute, then headed straight for Uncle Hank.

Jessie held her breath. Was the sheriff going to tell Uncle Hank that his newest cowhand, James, was a girl?

She caught Dexter's eye and knew he was wondering the same thing. She knew the idea worried him, too. Uncle Hank would have Dexter's hide for playing such a trick on him!

"James!" Uncle Hank called, turning to look at her.

She almost dropped the coffeepot.

"Come over here for a minute, will you?" he said. As usual, he was frowning.

Jessie gulped. She walked over to Uncle Hank with her head hanging, sure that in a matter of minutes she was going to be riding Smokey home in disgrace.

But she was wrong.

Changing Weather

The sheriff here tells me you're quite the roper," said Uncle Hank. "Care to give me a demonstration of your skills?" He handed her a lasso and pointed to Dexter, who was way over by the campfire. "If you can rope my nephew from here, I could use your help today on roundup. We've got a lot of calves to gather and brand this morning."

Jessie's knees felt weak with relief, and also with fright. "Can I use my own rope?" she asked.

Uncle Hank rolled his eyes. "Sure," he said.

Jessie ran to the chuck wagon for her lasso, then dashed back to Uncle Hank. She reached into her pocket and touched her lucky stone. Then, still breathing hard from her run, she started to twirl her rope. She sent it swirling out toward Dexter, who was facing away from her.

"What the —" Dexter cried as the rope settled around his shoulders. He turned to glare at Jessie.

Uncle Hank slapped his knee and burst into a guffaw.

Jessie was stunned. She'd never seen the man do anything but frown before!

"I'll tell Wiz he's on his own getting lunch ready today," Uncle Hank said, clapping her on the back. "We need a boy with your talent out on the range. Go get that paint cow pony of yours saddled up and be ready to ride when I give the word."

"But —" Jessie began. She had a million questions. But Uncle Hank was already striding off toward the chuck wagon.

Sheriff Gates gave Jessie a wink. "Have fun!" he told her as he threw a leg over his horse. "No need to worry about rustlers, anyway. Those three are all cozy in their new parlor, down at the county jail."

"Thank you!" was all Jessie could say. She hoped he understood how grateful she was for everything he had done, and for keeping her secret. She stood and watched him ride off. Then she ran for Smokey.

"Heard you're coming with us!" Dexter said with a big grin. "Better grab your slicker. We'll be getting rain by noontime, or I'm a monkey's uncle."

"You're a monkey yourself," teased Jessie as she swung up onto Smokey's back. She felt so happy, so alive. She couldn't have cared less if she got drenched to the skin. Let it rain! She was riding roundup. But Dexter was right. Dark clouds were gathering in the east, and the air was heavy and damp.

Uncle Hank gathered the hands to explain the day's plan. "We won't be moving camp today," he said. "We'll be riding circle, driving all the cattle we find back here. We'll cut out the calves and brand them, then drive the herd back to Chico's for the night."

Jessie knew that cutting out calves meant separating them from their mothers. It took a great horse and rider to get between a cow and her calf. Smokey was a terrific cutting horse. He could stop

short or turn on a dime, and he seemed to under-
stand without any directions just what Jessie
wanted him to do. They had practiced together
often enough in the corral at home. Now they
would have a chance to show off their teamwork
where it really counted.

First, Jessie and Dexter joined Pinky and Tiny,
riding far out into one wedge of the circle Uncle
Hank had described. The whole morning they
searched out all the Bar T cattle they could find,
including the ones that were hiding in gullies or in
thickets of mesquite.

Jessie knew that some of the cattle she was seeing were her father's. She could spot the Rocking
R brand a mile away. That meant that he and his
hands hadn't gotten to this part of the range yet.
She hoped they were working far, far away; the
last thing she needed was to run into anyone she
knew! Her days as a cowboy would be over in a
second if her father found out what she was up to.

Dexter, Jessie, Pinky, and Tiny worked all
morning, riding back and forth across their wedge
of the circle. They rounded up dozens of cattle and

calves. By the time they pushed those cattle back to the campsite, it was late afternoon. The sky was filled with towering dark clouds, and the air was thicker than ever. Jessie was starving by then, but Uncle Hank said there was no time to eat. "Grab a biscuit," he told the hands. "We'd best get our branding done right off, before the storm hits. The cattle are already getting jumpy."

"Tired?" Wiz asked when Jessie stopped at the chuck wagon.

"I'm exhausted," Jessie admitted as she accepted the biscuit he gave her and bit into it hungrily. "It's even harder work than cooking. But now the best part starts: cutting out the calves."

"Better take another biscuit if you're going to be doing that," Wiz said. "You'll need your energy."

He was right. Once the branding started, Jessie didn't have a second to rest. She and Smokey worked hard for hours, cutting bawling calves away from their mothers and roping them. Once her lasso had captured a calf, Jessie would slip off Smokey and tie the calf's legs with a leather strip known as a piggin' string. Smokey would brace himself to help hold the calf in place. Then another team would press the hot Bar T brand, fresh from the fire, into the left flank of each squirming animal. The second they were untied, the calves galloped straight back to their mothers' sides. A cow and her calf could find each other in the crowd by smell. They never, ever made a mistake.

Jessie was so caught up in the noisy, dusty work that she barely noticed when it began to rain. Big fat drops splooshed down into the dust, first one at a time and then in a torrent. The rain felt good on the back of Jessie's hot, sweaty neck.

"Faster, boys, faster!" yelled Uncle Hank, glancing up nervously at the sky. "That storm's going to let loose anytime now. We've got to get this herd into the canyon."

Finally, there were only ten calves left to brand, then eight, then five, then three. While Jessie helped Tiny cut out the last few, the rest of the hands began to gather the herd and get ready to move them toward Chico's Canyon.

Jessie was on her knees tying a piggin' string when she heard the first rumble of thunder.

"That's it!" cried Uncle Hank. "Leave the rest. Let's get these dogies moving — now!" He took off his hat and waved it at the herd of cattle. "Hyahh!" he cried. "Git along!"

Several cowboys moved to the back of the herd and began to push the cattle along. The big beasts began to trot, slowly at first and then more quickly, away from the campsite and toward Chico's Canyon. Jessie gave a sigh of relief. Without a doubt, this had been the longest, hardest day of work she had ever put in. She was glad it was almost over. She could smell biscuits baking and chili simmering in the magic kettle. It was nearly dusk now, though it felt even later because the sky was so very dark. It was almost time for a well-earned supper and rest. As soon as they got the cattle corralled in Chico's, they could relax.

Jessie joined the cowboys at the back of the herd, and soon Dexter slipped up next to her, riding Red. "Uncle Hank is really impressed," he told Jessie. "I heard him say you're the best young roper he ever saw."

Jessie grinned tiredly. "That's nice," she said.

A compliment from that sourpuss Uncle Hank was really something special. "But I'm not so sure I could do this every day for a whole week. I think I'll be glad when it's time to go back to being cook's helper."

She jogged along on Smokey's back feeling as if she could fall asleep in the saddle, she was so tired.

Then, suddenly, there was a clap of thunder that rattled her eardrums.

A bolt of lightning split the sky with a loud *crack*.

And in the next second, the cattle began to run.

"Stampede!" yelled Uncle Hank.

■ ■ ■

Molly, and everyone else, gasped. "Oh, no!" Molly said. Wasn't a stampede the worst thing that could happen? Jessie was really in trouble now.

"Well, I think we have to stop here," said Mr. Taylor, glancing at the clock. "After all, it's almost time for —"

"No!" said Molly. Her hand flew to her mouth. Had she really said that?

Mr. Taylor looked at her with raised eyebrows.

"I mean, *please*, Mr. Taylor. Please don't stop there. We *have* to know what happens next."

Mr. Taylor stroked his chin. "Hmm," he said. "Let's see. It's Friday. Are you all willing to do a little extra homework over the weekend to make up for missing a math period?"

"Yeah!" everyone shouted.

Well, everyone but Jason. He hated homework. But even Jason nodded. "Can't do anything else anyway," he mumbled, looking down at his cast.

"All right, then," said Mr. Taylor, settling back into his seat. "We'll go a little bit longer."

Stampede!

Suddenly, *the world was a blur of thundering hooves*, wild bellows, and wind-whipped rain. Jessie was terrified. "Dexter!" she shouted, but she couldn't even see him anymore. The rain was coming down in sheets, lit up every few seconds by a blinding flash of lightning.

The cattle were frantic with terror. Jessie could see the whites of their wildly rolling eyes whenever the lightning illuminated their faces. They tossed their big heads with their long, curled horns and bellowed into the sky as they ran. Their pounding hooves shook the earth beneath Smokey's feet; Jessie could feel the vibrations through her whole body.

"Head 'em off! Head 'em off!" Jessie heard Uncle Hank shouting. She didn't know what that meant.

But Smokey did.

Tired as he must have been from his long day's work, Smokey gathered his haunches beneath him and put on such a burst of speed that Jessie was thrown back in the saddle, holding on for dear life. The muscular little pony galloped alongside the herd until he had overtaken its leaders. Then he began to push the cattle back around so that the herd met itself coming and going and their desperate rush to nowhere was forced to stop. Jessie could hardly catch her breath when she saw what Smokey was doing. She helped him out by taking off her hat and waving it at the cattle. "Git along!" she yelled, just as she'd heard Uncle Hank do. "Git along!" By then she could see the shadowy figures of some other cowboys who had found their way to the front of the stampede. They were working hard to turn the cattle, too.

Jessie was holding on to her saddle horn with one hand and waving her hat with the other when Smokey lost his footing and slipped on the slick mud. He didn't fall — at the last moment he managed to stay upright. But Jessie lost her grip and slid right off her horse, right into the milling herd of cattle!

"Smokey!" she yelled. Her pony was already lost in the midst of the herd. "Help!" She was sure she was going to be trampled to death. Cattle loomed all around her, with their huge bodies and churning hooves. She could smell their hot, grassy breath and hear them panting with fear.

Then Smokey reappeared through the curtain of rain. He shouldered through the stampeding cattle, working his way back to Jessie. When he finally reached her side, he stretched his head down and snuffled softly into her ear, as if saying, "Come on, get up!" Jessie struggled to her feet but was knocked off balance by first one steer and then another pushing past her. "Help!" she yelled again.

Dexter appeared, high up on Red. He waved his hat at the cattle. "Heeyaw!" he yelled. "Get away!"

Their huge bodies parted for an instant, and Jessie jumped up and hauled herself onto Smokey's back.

"Are you all right?" Dexter asked between thunderclaps. The rumbling wasn't as loud now; the storm was moving away.

"I — I think so," Jessie said. She felt sore and bruised, but she could still move, couldn't she?

"I'm taking you back to camp," Dexter told her. "The stampede is turned, and the storm is dying down. The rest of the boys can get the cattle to the canyon. You might need some medical attention from Wiz."

"I said I'm fine!" Jessie said. But she wasn't. Now that she was settled on Smokey, she realized that her left arm was hanging at a strange angle, and she couldn't make it pick up the reins. It hurt, too. It hurt a lot.

■ ■ ■

"She broke her wrist, too!" yelled Jason. "It really does hurt. I can tell you that. At least until they put the cast on."

"But who's going to fix her up out there on the range?" Jennifer asked. "It's not like there's an emergency room handy, like there was for you."

"Shhh! Shh!" everybody else said. They were watching Mr. Taylor closely, waiting to hear what would happen next.

■ ■ ■

Suddenly, a figure on horseback approached. His broad silhouette was barely visible through the sheets of rain. "Uncle Hank?" Dexter asked.

The man shook his head. "Jessie," he said. "What on earth are you doing here?"

Jessie stared into his face. "Pa!" she sobbed.

Sent Home?

There, that ought to do you!" *Wiz nodded with satisfaction as he looked over his handi-work. He enjoyed the doctoring part of his job, that was plain. He'd gotten right to work on Jessie's wrist, as soon as her pa and Dexter had brought her back to camp. Jessie hadn't decided if it was a good or a bad thing that her dad had shown up. It had been both alarming and reassuring to hear his voice after the stampede was over. She still couldn't fathom what the chance was that her dad's outfit would show up in that stretch of the range at just that time.

Jessie looked at her arm. It was straight again now, and comfortingly cradled in a splint made of a couple of short planks wrapped with strips of cloth from an old tent. "It feels a lot better," she said. "Thank you."

"It'll be a few weeks before it's all healed up," Wiz warned her. "But if you take care of yourself, it'll be good as new before long. I broke my arm once when I was about your age, and I was climbing trees again in the blink of an eye." He smiled at Jessie and shook his head. "I had a feeling you weren't what you appeared to be," he said.

By then, every cowboy on roundup knew that Jessie was a girl. Pa had not kept quiet about the fact that James was actually his daughter. Wiz said he'd guessed it early on, but he didn't care as long as she pulled her weight. Uncle Hank, on the other hand, was flabbergasted when he heard the truth. But he was busy riding back and forth to the canyon, making sure the cattle were safe. He hadn't had time to say much yet.

"Your ma won't be happy about that arm," said Jessie's father. He had been at Jessie's side every second since appearing out of the rain. He had held her hand while Wiz set her broken arm and patted her back when she cried out in pain. "But she'll be glad to have you safe at home again."

"Home?" Jessie asked. "You mean, when roundup is over?"

Pa raised his eyebrows. "You don't think you're staying out here, do you? You aren't supposed to be here in the first place. Now that Dexter's uncle knows you're a girl, he'll never let you stay. Nor should he. That was some trick you pulled, missy." He shook his head, but he did not seem quite as angry as Jessie would have expected.

"I didn't meant to do anything wrong," Jessie said. "I — I just really wanted a chance to go out on roundup."

Pa nodded. "I know how badly you always wanted to do that," he said. "But what you did was wrong. It was a lie to pretend you were a boy."

Jessie decided this was not the time to tell him that the whole thing had been Ma's idea.

"But she's as good a hand as any of the others!" Dexter said. He had been there, too, watching Wiz set Jessie's broken bone. Jessie had noticed that his face had looked a little pale when he saw what Wiz had to do to make her crooked arm straight again.

"Ain't that the truth!" said Uncle Hank, who had just jumped off his horse and tied it to the chuck wagon. He shook Pa's hand. "You raised yourself quite a gal there. Wouldn't have believed it if I hadn't seen it with my own eyes, but she can ride and rope with the best of 'em. Never saw any young cowboy handle his first stampede so well! She's a real horsewoman."

"That may be," Pa said. "But her riding and roping days are over for now. I'll be taking her home tomorrow so her ma can nurse her."

"I don't need any nursing!" said Jessie. "I want to stay. Maybe I can't ride anymore, but I can still help Wiz." She waved her good arm in the air and looked from her Pa, to Wiz, to Uncle Hank. "Please?" she begged.

"I'm game," said Wiz. "And I sure could use the help. After all, I hired you because I can't cook for all these hands by myself."

"It's true, Pa," Jessie said. "Wiz needs me, and I agreed to work the roundup. You wouldn't want me to go back on my word, would you?"

"Well," Pa said slowly, considering this. "I suppose your ma isn't expecting you back yet. But it's up to the chief here to decide if you can stay."

Uncle Hank looked at Jessie and stroked his chin. "Let me sleep on it," he said. "I've never had a girl on roundup before, and I'm not sure I'm ready to start now."

"But, Uncle Hank," Dexter said, "you've had a girl on roundup for two days! You just didn't know it. What's the difference?"

Uncle Hank frowned at Dexter.

So did Jessie. Uncle Hank had to make up his own mind, and it wouldn't help to push him.

Dexter got the message. "Never mind," he said. "I'll go make sure the horses are settled."

"I'll go with you," said Jessie. She could hardly stand to wait until morning to find out if she'd be allowed to stay.

■ ■ ■

Mr. Taylor stopped. "But I'm afraid that you will all have to wait until Monday," he said.

Everybody groaned.

He held up his hands. "Sorry," he said. "That's the way it is. You have lunch now, then music, then library work. The rest of your day is all booked up."

The Hoop Shoot

Molly hardly ate a thing at dinner that night. Her mom had made macaroni and cheese, her favorite. But it might as well have been cardboard. She ate about three bites and put her fork down.

Her mother opened her mouth, then closed it again. She knew why Molly wasn't eating.

They all knew.

Because they were all going with her, over to the school gym, in about — Molly glanced at the clock for the fortieth time since she'd sat down to dinner — eight minutes.

Molly knew she had never been so nervous in her life. But she also felt strangely calm. She had agreed to be in the Hoop Shoot contest, and she was going to follow through. Just like Jessie followed through, even when things got hard or scary.

"You'll do great," Matthew said as they walked out to the car.

"You're the best," Mark told her as they arrived at the school.

"We'll be right there, watching," said her mother as they headed into the gym.

"Go get 'em," Stan urged as he thumped her on the back.

Her father didn't say anything. He just gave Molly a hard, quick hug right before he and the rest of her family climbed into the bleachers, leaving Molly standing there on the gym floor.

The contest started with an announcement about the rules. Participants would each get two forty-five-second rounds to make as many baskets as they could, from special spots marked on the gym floor. Each spot had its own point value. At the end, the shooter with the most points would win.

Molly tried to forget that her heart was beating like a big bass drum and her hands were sweating so much it would be hard to hold on to a basket-ball. She looked over the spots marked on the floor and planned her strategy. She knew she could make a lot of the harder shots and get more points that way.

Then she looked around at the rest of the contestants. There were some really little kids. They had their own contest since most of them couldn't throw the ball all the way up to the basket. There was a special little kids' basket set up at one end of the court.

The rest of the kids, the third through fifth graders, were warming up. Molly joined them, trying hard to focus on the ball, the basket, the stripes painted on the floor, anything but the faces and bodies filling the bleachers.

Then the contest began. And after that, every-thing was a blur for Molly. Later, she could recall a few moments — when Mimi Weathers sank a three-pointer from beyond the foul line, and when Steven Gross missed seven shots in a row. But she could barely remember her own first round. She only knew that she had tied for high score with Timmy Wackernagel, a big, tall fifth grader who was famous for having size eleven shoes.

During the second round, Timmy's friends were rooting hard for him. "Timmy! Timmy! Timmy!" they chanted when he started his shots. The referee called for quiet, and Timmy made shot after shot, from every spot on the floor. He only missed one, a seemingly easy shot from the right side of the key.

Molly's turn came last. By then, the only other person who had a score close to hers and Timmy's was a girl named Florence who had just moved to town. She was a good shooter, but she missed a few of the harder shots.

"Molly! Molly! Molly!" She heard everyone shouting her name. Molly took a deep breath. She glanced up at the bleachers and caught Mark's eye. He gave her a big wave. Next to Mark sat Molly's father. She had never seen him smiling quite like that before.

Molly knew that her classmates and Mr. Taylor

were sitting on the other side of the gym, high up in the top row of the bleachers. She could hear Jennifer shrieking her name. But Molly didn't look up there. She couldn't. If she thought too much about the fact that everyone was watching her, she would sprint out of the gym and run all the way home.

Instead, she took a few deep breaths. She let the crowd, the noise, everything fall away. She thought again about her strategy — which shots she would try to make. And then the buzzer went off, and it was time to start shooting.

Molly made shot after shot. She couldn't believe the way the ball was behaving. It seemed to find its way to the basket without any help from her. Once it bobbled on the rim, then dropped in anyway. Another time it seemed to sail way too high, but it arced at the last minute and swished through the net.

She wasn't keeping count of her score, but Molly knew she was doing well by the hush that had fallen over the gym. As she made her last few shots, the gym grew quieter and quieter.

The buzzer went off just as her last shot bounced off the backboard and dropped into the basket.

And then the gym exploded in cheers.

Molly had won the Hoop Shoot!

She looked down at her feet and felt her face grow hot. Suddenly, the old familiar shyness was washing over her again. She had to get out of there!

Timmy Wackernagel was giving her a high five. The principal was striding out onto the gym floor to shake her hand. Her friends from room 3B were surrounding her. Tall Mr. Taylor's smiling face loomed over the crowd. It was almost too much for Molly.

And then her family was there. Mark, and Stan, and Matthew. Her mom, who seemed to be crying a little. And her dad. "I'm so proud of you," he whispered into her ear as he swept her up into a big hug.

The End

You were awesome!" Jennifer said to Molly on Monday morning.

"Totally," agreed Jason. "Man, I think you would have even beat me!"

Molly blushed. She started to look down at the ground, and then she stopped. She made herself look right into Jennifer's eyes. "Thanks," she said. She knew she'd always be at least a little bit shy, but now she was more than just "the shy girl." Now she was also "that girl who won the Hoop Shoot for Mr. Taylor's class." And, it turned out, that felt great. She smiled at Jason, too. "I hope you get to enter next year's contest," she told him.

Mr. Taylor gave Molly a huge grin and led the class in a round of applause. "Can't wait to get that new computer!" he said. "We owe you a big thank-you for that."

"And we have to decide what kind of PJs Mr. Connor will have to wear," Cricket added. "I'm thinking something pink and frilly."

Molly had another idea, and for once she wasn't going to be shy about saying so. After all, who had won the contest? "I saw some Spider-Man pajamas at the store the other day," she said.

"Should we decide this now, during sharing time?" Mr. Taylor asked.

"Not today!" Molly said. "We have to finish Jessie's story! Does she get to stay on roundup or not?" Even if everybody else had forgotten, she hadn't.

"Let's go find out," Mr. Taylor suggested, leading the way to the reading corner.

■ ■ ■

Jessie stretched and rubbed her eyes. It was still dark out, but there was a band of blue and pink along the eastern horizon where the sun would soon show its face. She sat up and climbed out of her bedroll. As she rolled it up, Jessie wondered if this would be the last time she would ever do that task, the first morning duty of every cowboy on roundup. What if she had to spend the rest of her life working inside? She didn't think she could bear it. She loved being out on the range. Despite the backbreaking work and the scary stampede, roundup was more fun than she had ever imagined.

Jessie touched the lucky stone in her pocket for the millionth time since last night. If there was ever a time she needed good luck, it was now.

Across the fire, Dexter stirred and sat up. Their eyes met. He gave her a hopeful smile. Jessie knew he would be really sad to see her go if Uncle Hank told Pa to take her home.

When Jessie arrived at the chuck wagon, Wiz was already pulling the first batch of biscuits out of the Dutch oven they'd baked in. "Hey, there," he said. "What are you doing up so early?"

"I came to help with breakfast," Jessie said. "Isn't that what I was hired on for?" She shrugged and smiled. "I know I left you on your own yesterday so I could help with roundup, but with this broken wing I can't ride anymore, so here I am again!"

Wiz smiled. "I missed your help yesterday,

James — I mean, Jessie." He handed her a big spoon. "Think you can stir up that gravy one-handed?"

"I sure can!" said Jessie. She headed off to the cook fire.

When she returned, Uncle Hank and Pa were standing by the chuck wagon, drinking their first mugs of coffee and talking with Wiz.

"Wiz here says he could sure use your help, even with that busted arm," said Uncle Hank. "I'm still not sure it's a good idea, but the boys are counting on good grub. They need plenty of food to keep them going, and Wiz can't do it alone." He paused for a moment. "So what do you say? Want to stay on through roundup?"

Jessie looked at Pa. "May I?" she asked.

Pa hesitated.

"Please, Pa?" Jessie begged.

"All right," he said. "On one condition."

Jessie guessed just what he was thinking. "I know," she said. "You want me to promise I'll never beg to go on roundup again, now that I've had my chance."

Pa grinned. "Nope," he said. "I want you to promise you'll work for the Rocking R crew next year. We need a hand like you!"

● ● ●

Mr. Taylor stopped.

Was that the end?

Molly couldn't stand it. She had loved Jessie's story. She didn't want it to be over. But then she remembered something. "Hey!" she said, without even raising her hand. "What about the penny?" Her fifth item hadn't even been mentioned. Had Mr. Taylor forgotten all about it?

Mr. Taylor smiled. "You don't miss a thing, do you?" he asked. "Well, I was just getting to that."

● ● ●

About a week after roundup ended, Dexter and Wiz rode over to the Rocking R Ranch one afternoon. Jessie's ma invited them in for coffee, and Wiz settled into a chair at the kitchen table between Slim and Pa.

After they'd all talked a bit, Wiz slid a heavy envelope across the table to Jessie.

"What's this?" Jessie asked as she slit it open.

"Your pay," said Wiz. "Remember? We hired you on to work this roundup. You earned every cent."

"A rich woman!" Slim crowed. "Now you'll never sell me that horse. You don't need the money!"

"Oops!" Jessie cried as the envelope tore open. Bills fluttered through the air, and coins rattled onto the wooden floor. Dexter laughed and helped Jessie scramble for the money.

"I think that's all of it," said Jessie as she stuffed her pay — the first money she'd ever earned — back into the envelope.

"Nope!" said Dexter. He pointed to a penny that had rolled under the lion's-claw foot of Ma's iron cookstove. "I'll get it." He got down on his hands and knees and started to crawl toward it. "It's heads up!" he reported when he got nearer. "That means good luck, doesn't it?" Jessie had taught him all her good-luck signs.

"Wait!" said Jessie, before he could pick it up. "I think I've had all the good luck I need for a little while. Let's leave it for someone else to find."

"And so they left it," said Mr. Taylor. "And you know the funny thing? Nobody did find that penny, not for a long, long time. Not for more than fifty years! Then one day, a boy was out west on vacation with his parents. They visited a museum, an old restored ranch called the Double Bar T. They looked at all the exhibits of cowboy clothes and gear, different types of barbed wire, and a restored chuck wagon. The boy loved everything he saw because he loved learning about cowboys and how they lived. When he and his parents were touring the ranch house kitchen, he dropped his favorite marble. It rolled under the cookstove, and when he knelt down to rescue it he spotted a penny under the lion's-claw foot. It was an old one, too. The woman who ran the museum let him keep it as a souvenir."

Mr. Taylor stuck his hand into his pocket. "Here it is!" he said, pulling out an old copper penny. "This penny sure has brought me plenty of good luck." He gave Molly a special look, and she knew just what he was thinking. Mr. Taylor felt lucky to have her as a student! And not just because she had won the Hoop Shoot, either.

For once, Molly didn't blush or stare down at her shoes. She just smiled right back at Mr. Taylor. She knew she was lucky, too.

About the Author

Ellen Miles has always loved a good story. She also loves biking, skiing, writing, and playing with her dog, Django. Django is a black Lab who would rather eat a book than read one.

Have **Mr. Taylor's** students finally stumped **him?**

Jason thinks he knows how to really puzzle Mr. Taylo[r] when he picks items from a[ll] around the globe that would neve[r] be found together. A polar bea[r] and a penguin? No way! Will M[r]. Taylor be able to fit them bot[h] into one fascinating story[?]

Find out in *Taylor-Mad[e] Tales #4*, the nex[t] book in the series[.]

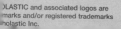

SCHOLASTIC
www.scholastic.com

LITTLE APPLE